Are You Crazy?

미치셨어요?

WRITTEN BY SNOW

EDITIO

PUBLISHING

Are You Crazy?

© SNOW

Cover Illustration by Poya

This is a work of fiction. Names, characters, businesses, places, events, locales, and incidents are either the products of the author's imagination or used in a fictitious manner. Any resemblance to actual persons, living or dead, or actual events is purely coincidental.

The views and opinions expressed in this work are those of the author and do not necessarily reflect the views and opinions of Editio Publishing, LLC.

미치셨어요? by SNOW

This English edition was published by Editio Publishing LLC in 2025 by exclusive contract with Kyobo Book Centre Co. Ltd.

ISBN 978-1-959742-62-3 (Print)

Printed in the United States of America

https://editiopublishing.com/

EDITIO

PUBLISHING

Are You Crazy?

CONTENTS

CHAPTER
FORTY-ONE

"That's why Eid is paying such a huge price," Shea said.

"Oh? So, you do pity him?" Noise replied. "I thought you hated him."

"Hating him doesn't change my assessment of the situation. You agree with me, don't you?"

"He really is a world-class moron, but it'll be difficult to find anyone more unfortunate than him." Noise added, quite unnecessarily, that Eid must have done something atrocious in his past life to deserve this fate.

"The nonsense that I had to go through because of him prevents me from liking him," Shea said, "but I do pity him."

"Understandable. I was shocked the first time I saw you raising Elias. You? People like us, raising kids? It's hard to believe."

They'd all been born with a terrible fate.

Shea frowned. "Did you actually consider having children to pass down this terrible fate?"

"Are you crazy? I haven't gone *that* insane yet." Noise looked appalled by the idea.

Shea couldn't find it in her to laugh at him, even though it was funny to hear someone so crazy say this. He sounded too genuine.

"We're all the same. That's why we rarely ever pass on our names, even when we adopt someone."

"I'd love a smoke." Shea rubbed her thumb and forefinger together at the sudden urge.

Edward, who didn't know Shea smoked but was well aware this wasn't a conversation for him to butt into, sprang to his feet before he could stop himself. "You smoke?"

As if he didn't.

Noise responded for Shea, who appeared surprised by the interruption. "Of course not. Shea can't stand the sight of anyone smoking. She'd punch anyone who smoked in front of her." *It's like you don't even know her.*

Edward was immediately convinced. It sounded exactly like something Shea would do.

"But what about—"

"Oh, she was talking about a sedative for her nerves. It's a specialized blend for Shea. She hated taking medicine, so she had it made into a form of cigarette. Shea calls it smoking because she's too lazy to explain. Got it?"

Shea cleared her throat. "Right. So, sit back down, Edward, it's embarrassing." She pointed at Noise. "And you, stop teasing my boyfriend."

"Come on, I was just getting started!"

She waved away his whining. "Stop it. I can't be bothered to console him later."

"What kind of girlfriend are you? I feel bad for him."

"Shut up. Do you want me to make you feel bad for yourself?"

"No, thank you, of course not. You know me. I still have so much to live for."

The way Noise adjusted to her moods made him look like a docile dog. Edward sat back down and let Elias onto his lap again.

Shea tried to wrap up the conversation. "So, you're here to eat all my food and say hi?"

"That's right."

"Lucy, go and get some salt and throw it at him," she called. "Preferably on his face."

"Hey, that's painful!"

"That's exactly why I do it."

Noise grumbled and got to his feet. "In any case, I'm overjoyed to see that we still think alike."

"We always do. Why did you even have to check?"

They had been used and lost so much. Their intent and wishes were always the same, never changing. She asked why he would doubt that, and he smiled.

Shea recalled a bad memory with a frown. "I kept telling him that he would regret it."

"The young ones are all like that. Not that they get any more mature with age."

Shea nodded at his sharp observation. She knew herself very well.

Noise, who knew exactly why she agreed with him so easily, glanced over at Edward. "Are you sure you won't regret it? I thought you would be sick of it by now."

Shea responded with a scoff, as if he were asking something ridiculous. "Life is an endless loop of regrets. If it were you in my shoes, you'd make the same decisions, as well."

Noise burst out laughing at her clear, confident answer. He approached her with a pleased expression, then leaned in and placed a light kiss on her lips.

Everyone rubbed their eyes in disbelief at the scene before them.

"...!"

"Whoa."

"What the heck?"

Cheating right in front of her boyfriend? As audacious as some nobles were, this wasn't something they could easily imagine. Perhaps Shea really was on a different level.

As everyone around them came up with wild theories, Shea sat still, letting him kiss her as if it were nothing.

The customers were unable to get any more upset—since she didn't seem to care. The two people in question were in their own world.

She smiled at Noise. "I wish you continual happiness, brother of my people, my beloved family."

"Same to you. Always, my bonded one, my unity, my only one."

Everyone watched this reverent scene with bated breath.

The playful smile from earlier reappeared on Noise's face as he waved at Shea. "See you again!"

She waved back. "Isn't it better for us not to see each other?" No news was good news, after all.

"We'll see each other soon, anyway. It's time for the song soon."

"Already?" *I see. It's already that time again. I suppose that's good.* She smiled faintly.

Noise grinned with childlike glee. "See you later, Shea!"

"Sure."

It was an unusual goodbye and an unusual exit.

That same day, the news that one of the guardian stones had been broken reached Eid's ears.

"It's broken?"

"Yes," Ace replied. "Duke Maxwell has confirmed that the northern ward has been removed, along with the power of the Emerald of the North. There has been an unprecedented cold front, the likes of which we haven't seen in hundreds of years, which makes it very obvious."

"How bad is the damage right now?"

"All the water pipes in the North have frozen and burst, and the crops have wilted due to the sudden change in weather. There are reports of people freezing in a type of cold they've never felt before."

It had been nearly a thousand years since such a cold front hit the empire. The North had always been colder than the rest, but there had never been such severe storms or drops in temperature drastic enough to leave it inhospitable. Nothing could withstand the sudden freeze in a region accustomed to mild winters.

"Request assistance from the mages living in the North, and have them deal with the cold—"

"We already have. They've used magic items to help with the basics, but with the ward gone, monsters have been invading. We've received reports that the mages are too busy dealing with them to focus on the cold. There are requests for aid and a quick solution to this issue."

Eid furrowed his eyebrows in frustration.

The Vencroft Empire had always enjoyed a mild climate. Ambassadors from other countries visiting the North were always shocked by how mild the weather was there. There were hardly any measures in place to handle even a normal cold front. The weather conditions have always been predictable so far. In fact, there had never been severe cold fronts anywhere in the empire, so no preventive measures or solutions existed.

The same went for monster invasions. Citizens were rarely attacked by a monster unless they lived on the outskirts or went into monster-infested woodlands.

Vencroft was not prepared for the situation at hand. It was laughable for such a great empire to be so unprepared.

"Hmm, what in the world is a guardian stone?" Eid mused. "Is it that important?"

Ace blinked, astonished that the emperor would ask such a question. "Are you serious?"

Eid's eyebrows furrowed. "Tell me."

The emperor himself didn't know. *You barbarian. Are you sure you're a Vencroft?*

Though knowledge of the guardian stones was now only passed down as a legend, since so much time had passed, it was crucial knowledge for the imperial family, the three duchies, and the families protecting the borders. Maybe this was why people said history didn't matter. Everyone changed it to their liking, in the end. It was probably why they had no sense of guilt whatsoever as they reinterpreted history according to their wants and needs.

People were all the same.

"Do you even know that there are four guardian stones in the empire?" Ace asked.

"That's enough."

Ace immediately backed off, scrambling for a simple explanation that wouldn't annoy the emperor. "As you learned in your history lessons, Lucid Roux Vencroft, the first emperor and founder of the empire, was said to have been chosen by Roux to found Vencroft."

"A bunch of made-up talk to make the imperial family look good."

"Be that as it may, Lucid Roux Vencroft was said to have founded the empire with the help of those given special abilities by Roux, the Children of God. Then he asked Roux for a favor."

CHAPTER
FORTY-TWO

Even a man appointed by Roux couldn't found a nation alone.

Admittedly, there were others who helped. And since this was something even hundreds of ordinary humans wouldn't be able to accomplish, Lucid asked someone special: those who'd been blessed with God-given abilities since the beginning of time.

It was surprising how easily he found them. Scholars later said that it was thanks to Roux' blessing. In any case, the first emperor convinced the Children of God to help him and founded his nation without any issues.

But the promise they made with the first emperor was to found the nation together, to allow the nation to exist. They couldn't be pinned down forever. Once the nation was founded, they went their separate ways. Although Lucid tried to find them again, he was never able to, as if the blessing he received had run its course.

He was frustrated. Founding a nation wasn't all there was to it. It had to be ruled properly, and diplomatic relations had to be established with neighboring nations. The process was arduous, making something out of nothing.

He cried out to the Great God Roux in desperation, "You tasked me with founding this nation—I ask that you give me the strength to protect it. Have mercy on this fledgling nation."

Back then, Vencroft was not the abundant land it was today. It was plagued with monsters, and fertile soil was scarce—what little there was proved unsuitable for most crops. There was no specific reason for choosing this land, but it was too late for second thoughts. The nation had been hastily established on the land that was available.

Lucid was desperate for help. He had no one to turn to. His helplessness and desperation touched Roux' heart, so Roux bestowed a gift upon the emperor. Actually, it was a person: the first child, one of the individuals who helped Vencroft found the nation.

The Child of God appeared before the first emperor, looking extremely annoyed. "It is only natural that the nation be unstable at first. Overcoming this was your job." He criticized Lucid for agreeing to found a nation and become its ruler despite lacking the will to do so.

While Lucid understood his annoyance, he felt wronged. "This instability is not something I can overcome on my own. I don't have your superhuman powers, either. Why did you leave me? This nation still needed you, and you were a founder, along with me. So why did you not help?"

The Child of God looked at Lucid, exasperated that he spoke as though he took their help for granted. "We only agreed to found the nation with you." *So why do you ask for more? Will you give up your status as ruler? You will go insane with paranoia, imagining that we are planning to overthrow you.*

When the Child of God spoke nothing but the truth, Lucid found himself speechless. He had no extraordinary skills. He was no benevolent hero able or willing to save the world, nor did he have the raw charisma to attract skillful individuals to work for him. He was an ordinary man—a perfectly average, weak man.

The Children of God had departed for his sake. As much as they knew him, having spent time with him, he could also tell that they had indeed been watching out for him when they left. They had always been kind in their coldness.

He begged the Child of God on his knees. "Give me strength, the power to protect. I and this nation are far too weak."

The Child of God sighed deeply at the sight of him. "None of us will help you. We have no reason or responsibility to do so. This will not change, no matter how much you beg. Human greed is limitless, and you will fail to change."

"…"

Lucid had nothing to say. He couldn't deny it. All he could do was grit his teeth.

The Child of God spoke again. "Therefore, this will be the last time. The last time I help you or this nation."

"…!"

"Helping you will be the death of me, so continuing to beg afterward will not work."

"That's—"

"What? Do you suddenly feel bad? Then refuse. If you can't refuse my help, don't even pretend to feel bad. Your hypocrisy makes me want to change my mind. Your petty ways of making yourself feel better make me nauseous."

Lucid closed his mouth obediently at the sharp criticism.

The Child of God smiled, seemingly pleased by his obedience. "I cannot promise eternity, but it will last a long time. You won't need to worry for at least a few generations. That is my last gift to you. If you happen to come across my siblings in your lifetime, greet them for me."

And with that, the Child of God infused his life energy into four gems and placed them at each border. Those who served him were stationed there as guardians of these guardian stones, which had persisted since that time.

Ace turned to Eid. "The stones are the emerald at the northern border, the ruby at the southern border, the topaz at the western border, and the diamond at the eastern border. Together, they create a ward. Vencroft became a land of milk and honey where there are no droughts, no floods, and no invasions from monsters or enemies."

Eid nodded. "In other words…"

"Yes, everything we enjoy is thanks to that ward. There have been incidents here and there because the ward has weakened as time has passed, but it is still powerful." Even if they tried as hard as they could, Ace added, they wouldn't be able to come up with anything even close to the power of the stones.

Eid, who had listened closely to Ace's cynical summary, scoffed. "So, it's finally falling to ruin."

"Sire, this is your empire."

"Since when did Vencroft belong to me? I am nothing but a single component of this empire."

"I suppose you're not wrong. But you are aware that there's no one who can take your place, aren't you?"

Eid nodded. "That's why I said it's finally falling into ruin. This nation should've fallen a hundred times over already."

Throughout its long history, Vencroft had faced numerous opportunities to fall into ruin. Each time, it had endured because a member of the imperial family sacrificed themselves to prevent it. This had also occurred during Eid's lifetime.

Ace, who knew the truth beyond what Eid remembered, choked up. The memories forming in his head made it worse.

"I hope it works, Ace."

"You're working hard."

"I respect your decision. Please watch after him for me."

The flickering light in his head made him squeeze his eyes shut.

He was a sinner. He had committed a sin that could never be forgiven. The price he had to pay was only natural, perhaps even too little. In all honesty, he still regretted it. If he had stepped down from the throne like he'd wished to and they hadn't had to pay the price, the two of them would have been—

"Ace."

But it was too late. He couldn't turn back time.

"But since it hasn't fallen yet," Ace said. "We must do our best."

He couldn't let Vencroft be destroyed. His life had been extended by unspeakable means. When he thought of the price they had to pay, he couldn't let it go.

"Is that you being considerate?"

"It may be more like a curse, but please don't mind it. Let's discuss our next steps."

"What a pity." *I would prefer the empire to fall.*

It was clear how much Eid resented his position and wished to be rid of his title. Ace nearly gave in to the compulsion to tell him everything. *How could you say that? Do you know what you have lost for the sake of the nation?*

He wanted to cry out and tell him, but he couldn't. He— no, no one who knew the truth had any right to tell him about it. Ace had been the one to convince him, so he had no right.

"Let's get back to work." *You may be able to let go, but I could never. You sacrificed too much. We can't let it end here.*

Eid turned his attention to the reports on his desk. "Keep an eye on the temple."

"Why?"

"A sudden catastrophe is the perfect chance for them to run wild."

Ace, who hadn't thought that far ahead, was immediately convinced. He quickly relayed the order, then quietly excused himself.

Eid watched him as he left. His expression softened as he mumbled to himself. "You're still bad at lying."

Your guilty conscience is far too obvious. You know... I don't know what it is, but I feel like I do. Why does it feel so unpleasant?

Eid frowned as he leaned back in his chair.

"Eid."

There it was. *Again.*

"You look tired."

A voice that he was sure he didn't know yet tugged at his heartstrings.

"You're so lovely."

Eid's hunch was correct.

The temple did not miss this opportunity. They began to proselytize enthusiastically in order to gain more followers—that was, slaves.

"The biggest catastrophe in Vencroft's history is about to befall us, because Roux' blessing that was bestowed upon us in the beginning is running out. It is running out because the people's faith has weakened. Everyone! The Great God Roux is always with you. Be one with his will! Join us, who serve him. With Roux' blessing, we swear that the temple will always sacrifice itself for the peace of the people."

"Huh?"

"Are they trying to proselytize?"

Naturally, because everyone knew about the temple's past nefarious activities, the priests' proselytizing didn't appear entirely innocent.

CHAPTER FORTY-THREE

Crowd sentiment was as easily swayed as reeds in the wind.

"Do you think they're right, though?"

"Of course not. Then again, based on what we hear from the North..."

While they were well aware of the temple's misdeeds, the undeniable reality of a momentous cold front and monster attacks were persuasive. A worried heart is easily convinced.

The priests must have been using magic items to amplify their voices, because their preaching reached the ears of those inside Sangria. Shea would have never gone to listen herself.

She had only one thing to say as she watched the priests yell.

"They're great at spewing bullshit."

The nobles gathered at Sangria pressed their lips together to keep from laughing.

"Pfft."

"Don't laugh! Pfft."

With Elias in her arms, Shea grimaced and turned to Lucy. "Alert the guards and tell them to take those lowlifes away. They're disrupting my business. This is noise pollution."

After downgrading her characterization of the priests' ardent preaching, she took Elias upstairs.

Thanks to her dismissive appraisal, the potentially fear-inducing speech now sounded trivial, and those at Sangria were able to laugh at the situation. But that didn't mean they didn't recognize the severity of the situation. The regulars at Sangria were those who led the nation.

"I suppose some people will be convinced."

"Not just some. As soon as the masses begin to sway, the temple's influence will be enormous."

"I guess so. His Imperial Majesty is probably keeping an eye on them."

Shea was also fully aware of the situation. Even though she'd dismissed it as noise pollution, she wasn't stupid enough to dismiss the seriousness of it all.

"This is going to get ugly."

I might die of annoyance. All I want is to live a quiet life.

Meanwhile, Edward was up to his neck in urgent work. The

temple's proselytizing was a catastrophe for the imperial palace—no, for all of Vencroft. If they weren't stopped, they would grow to an overwhelming, uncontrollable size.

"Sir, this is the budget proposal from the department of finance."

"Here are the planning documents from the prime minister."

"Add it to the pile!"

"Sir, there've been reports from the Maxwell territory, and—"

"There are requests for backup from the North."

"What about this?"

"And this!"

Though most departments were swamped with work and requests, due to the nature of the situation, the Ministry of Defense was affected the most. And among the officials, it was the Minister of Defense who suffered most.

Edward felt like he might die. Since the actual Minister of Defense was absent, he was the one being badgered instead. There was so much work that he thought he might faint. He barely had time to use the bathroom, let alone meet his lover. Though he hadn't had a chance to express it, he wanted to find his father, capture him, and throw him back into his seat as minister, where he belonged, so that he could escape.

Damn you, father.

It wasn't like he could quit—since it wasn't his job to begin with. It was worse because he'd been forced into the position as his father's substitute. If he quit now, the tyrant would threaten his life.

Edward didn't even entertain the idea. In the past, a death threat wouldn't have fazed him, but things were different now. He needed to survive. He now had someone who made him want to live.

"Cheshire."

"You cannot."

"I didn't even say anything yet."

"Whatever it is, you cannot." Cheshire's glare was pointed, as if he felt extremely wronged. *How dare you even think about running away when I wasn't able to, either?*

Edward gave up when he saw Cheshire's menacing glare. *I guess I can't dump my workload on him today.*

It wasn't the kind of work he could dump on anyone else. When even his small hope was dashed, Edward felt depressed. A completely unexpected miracle had happened in his life, and his heart had been elated. If it really was a dream, he never wanted to wake up, even if that meant going crazy or dying.

This was his first time liking someone this much, the first time his heart had fluttered, the first time he'd found himself completely helpless. For some reason, he turned into a fool in front of Shea, a fool who was completely incompetent, could hardly get a word out, and could only cling to her.

Ever since he first met her...

"..."

...his heart had raced like never before, and he'd been unable to turn his eyes away. It was as if his whole body was focused on her.

As if this wasn't the first time.

As if the universe were telling him that he couldn't miss this chance.

It was almost instinct. That's why he went to see her every time he got the chance. Even though she rejected him and pushed him away, even though he couldn't talk to her, he couldn't stand being away from her. He followed her around like a puppy, continuously, without giving up. He never grew tired of going to see her.

That was still the case.

"Do you like her that much?" Cheshire asked.

"Of course I do."

Even now, he was nearly panicking with every passing day. Not being able to see her made him anxious. And seeing her made him ecstatic. Only when he was next to her did he feel alive.

And again...

"...?"

...he feared losing her.

"Sir?"

What was that thought just now? Losing her? He suddenly felt nauseated.

"What?" He could swear that he hadn't known her before. They'd never met in the past. They'd been worlds apart, even though they were from the same city. There hadn't been a chance for them to meet, and even if they had, it didn't make sense for him to feel like he had lost her.

Losing her? There hadn't been another woman before her, either. So why did he keep getting this strange feeling? He couldn't understand it.

"Let's go and find the duke immediately. Working too much is bad for you." Cheshire must have been affected by the way Edward suddenly looked flustered and lost.

But Edward was deaf to this idea, which he would have welcomed gladly a moment ago. It felt like his brain had been scrambled.

Never. You should never lose her.

As if another part of him was whispering to him.

"Sir?"

"I have to go," Edward said.

It whispered to him that he must not lose her.

"All right," Cheshire said, "but you must be back by evening."

Not this time.

"What's with this mountain of macarons?"

Shea usually never worked this hard. Lucy was stunned at the sight of a colorful mountain of what were easily hundreds of beautiful macarons. The steadily increasing pile of macarons made no sense to her—when Shea seemed perfectly normal otherwise. *This is very unlike her.*

On a normal day, Shea would already have thrown down the mixing bowl because making meringue was such a hassle. Today, she was moving to and from while humming to herself, having already finished a dozen batches.

It was almost scary.

Even the customers, who would normally have crowded around the mountain of macarons like a pack of starving beasts, stayed seated while sipping their tea, shooting wary glances toward the kitchen. Shea was less scary when she was actually mad.

Unaware of or uninterested in what everyone was thinking, Shea kept making her macarons with a pleased expression. "It's sort of a... a bribe?"

She said it so casually—although there was nothing casual about it—that Lucy thought she had heard wrong. She stuck a finger into her ear.

Shea frowned, looking annoyed. "What, is it that weird?"

"Yes." *Do you really need to ask?*

Shea let out a huff of laughter at the almost offensively quick reply. "I guess I have to admit that this is unlike me."

"It's far more than that." Lucy explained that this was more akin to the sun rising from the west—or a sign of the apocalypse.

Shea burst out into laughter. "Pfft. Fine, it's weird. Even I think it's weird, and I'm the one doing it."

"So why are you doing it?"

"Because it doesn't suit me?" *I've never done something like this for him.*

Lucy frowned as if she couldn't understand what Shea was saying. "What do you mean?"

"I'm not sure myself."

I wonder why I've never done it for him. There were so many opportunities. It couldn't be explained by laziness or arrogance. She'd been stupid—and maybe she still was.

"Mistress?"

Shea straightened. "All right, this is probably enough. Let's pack them up. We have to get it done by today. There's no time."

Lucy shrugged, giving up on getting a straight answer. She picked up a gift wrap. "I'll do it, but... why are you doing this today?"

Shea gave her a playful smile. "I plan on doing something bad today."

"Something bad?"

"Yup. Let's hurry. There's no time."

She sounded like a child, proud of doing something mischievous.

"All right, everything's ready."

Though she'd boasted about doing something bad today, Shea couldn't be sure it would be today, after all. She didn't know when he would come by. She'd had a feeling it would be today, though, which was why she'd prepared all this. Some would've said she was being reckless.

But Shea didn't care.

CHAPTER
FORTY-FOUR

Shea had great faith in her gut feelings. She'd gotten into trouble so many times because of these damn gut feelings, and the scale of those troubles had been huge. It was probably the same for every one of her "siblings."

Though sometimes, she hated it.

"Hmm. How do I deliver this? You're supposed to give tributes in person."

Though she had no knowledge of giving presents or fangirling, she remembered a thing or two from the girls she'd known who had dedicated their entire bank accounts to their favorite celebs. She hadn't listened properly, though, so her memory was hazy. She knew the present should be delivered in person, but now that it came down to it, she found herself too embarrassed.

Ugh, this is so unlike me, but I've never done this before. This sucks.

She stared at the basket full of nicely wrapped macarons. *Should I go? Or not?*

Then something came to mind.

"Thank you."

The thought of him trying to act calm despite being overjoyed.

"Fine." She made up her mind. "Lucy, let's close the café early. Kick out this riffraff, and—"

The customers interrupted her with their objections.

"Shea!"

"This is tyranny!"

"The customer gets to choose when to leave!"

Shea frowned. "Give them each a macaron."

"..."

Everyone immediately shut up. Macarons were a delicacy she rarely ever made—because they were such a hassle.

As the customers left with their macarons, Shea continued instructing Lucy, "Take Elias and go to Grande for a while. I'll take care of the café."

"What? Why, all of a sudden—"

"I have a bad feeling."

Lucy, who was usually completely compliant with Shea's orders, seemed unenthusiastic about this sudden turn of events, so Shea told her about her gut feeling.

Shea usually never talked about her gut feelings. Knowing how accurate they were, though, Lucy found herself only able to nod. Shea's voice was firm but sad. Lucy knew very well that nothing she said would convince Shea otherwise, like the time Shea had rescued her without hesitation from that hell.

Shea gave Lucy a rare smile and warm hug. "Grande will always welcome you, so don't let yourself feel uncomfortable there. I have Fel with me, so don't worry."

"I know it's because you know he wouldn't leave, even if you ordered him to."

"You got me."

Lucy held back the tears that threatened to fall at the sound of Shea's chuckle and hugged her back tightly. "Can't I stay with you, too?"

"Who's going to take care of Elias, then?"

"There are plenty of nice people in Grande who would love to take care of him."

"Not as well as you do, though." *You love taking care of him the most.*

But when Lucy only hugged her tighter, Shea hugged her back and spoke in a voice so gentle it would have made Edward jealous. "I cherish you, Lucy."

"..."

"I really do." *Enough to not want you to die.*

Lucy, having understood Shea's feelings, squeezed back her tears. "Don't skip meals because I'm not here. You have to open the café regularly, all right? I don't want to come back to a destroyed building because you caused a riot."

"All right."

"You have to make at least three different things to sell every day, and you have to keep things tidy even if Fel is in charge of cleaning, and—"

"Lucy."

"A-and…"

"Lucy."

"And you have to come get us, okay?"

Shea smiled at Lucy, who was trying to act mature but was now allowing herself to act the child again. "Of course."

My lovely child.

Shea felt conflicted. Her son refused to cry or whine, even though it was clear that he didn't want to be apart from her.

She said goodbye to Lucy and Elias, wishing he'd whined maybe a little.

Even though she hadn't initially wanted to raise Elias. The way he took after his mother, despite not being related by blood, tugged at her heartstrings. Maybe it was her fault for raising him that way. She loved him very much, but she wasn't a good mother. She knew that much, at least. If his actual mother had raised him, he wouldn't have turned out like this. He would've acted more his age and become a lovely boy overflowing with affection.

Just like his mother.

"I never thought it would be easy, but it really isn't." One of the hardest things to do, they said, was to raise a child. It had turned out to be true. It was something you couldn't succeed at simply by trying hard—but you had to try hard.

It was a total mess.

She didn't know how to raise a child well or be a good mother. Then again, the standard of "well" or "good" was different for everybody, so maybe it was meaningless.

As Shea turned around in contemplation, Fel, always by her side like a shadow, made himself known.

"Would you have liked me to send you away, too?" she said with a sigh.

"Grande is certainly a good place to rest."

"It's not too late to go with them." With how fast he was, he'd be able to catch up with the carriage within ten minutes.

Fel let out a small chuckle at her joking but half-sincere suggestion. "You know the only reason I'm staying here is you."

"You're fond of Elias and Lucy, as well."

"They're lovely children. I didn't think I would feel this way again in my lifetime, so even more so."

"I know."

"No, you don't," he said firmly.

Shea suddenly found herself at a loss for words. "Fel."

"You're the one who made me the way I am." His words were calm but firm, making them sting even more.

Shea couldn't hold back a laugh as her heart twanged. *You really are...*

"The reason I'm still alive is because of you," he said.

"..."

"Don't forget that."

...hard to deal with. Especially because she didn't hate him.

She decided to throw in the towel. "Fine, fine. No one can stop you. It's not like I could win against you."

"Yes, you could."

Shea let out a sincerely exasperated laugh. "Who, me? Beat the former imperial knight captain?"

"That was ages ago."

"Fel. Fein Osborne. The immovable, unchanging master swordsman of Vencroft." The top swordsman in Vencroft, a nation reputed to have more sword masters than any other. A commoner who ascended through the ranks to become the empire's hero. The man who vanished as though he were merely a legend, once he reached the pinnacle.

That was the man standing in front of her.

The pitiful man who only ever wanted peace, not infinite wealth, or irrefutable power, and who had put down everyone and lost everything because of it. It had been a stroke of pure luck to have found him and taken him in.

"Fel."

"Yes?"

"Don't you miss them?"

Fel's smile changed into something different, a smile Shea herself had worn once. Faint and sad. "Always."

Forever.

She let out a chuckle at his unchanging answer. He would always be incorrigible like this.

Just like her.

And just like...

"I thought you might be waiting for me."

Shea looked up. "Wow. My gut feeling strikes again. It really is reliable."

"It's been a while, Shea."

"Same to you, Cedric Illid."

...this man.

"Welcome to Sangria," she added.

Again. There it is again.

Eid frowned. He hadn't been able to sleep lately. He'd always had trouble sleeping, but lately it had gotten worse. Though he'd never had dreams before, lately he'd been plagued by them. On top of that, the dreams seemed like memories of the past, starring himself.

Dreams where he watched himself. They were always different, yet similar. There was a woman he didn't know who kept appearing, and he was always with her.

"You didn't kill another person today, did you?" the woman demanded to know.

If any other woman had badgered him like this, he would have ignored her or even killed her if she grew too annoying. That's what women were to him.

But the Eid in his dreams treated her in a way that was exasperatingly different. "No, not today." He watched her warily, apparently nervous about how she would respond.

The sight of himself acting in such a way was baffling, even though it was a dream.

But the woman in the dream looked like she was used to this and let out a long sigh. "I'm not sure whether I should get angry at the 'not today' part or be happy about your progress."

"Where did you learn that attitude?"

"From my friend. She must have rubbed off on me when I went to see her yesterday, on my day off."

Only then did Eid notice what she was wearing. It was the uniform not of an attendant but of a lowly maid, the kind of uniform given to those who worked at the imperial palace part time and had no status whatsoever. A job anyone from any background could do.

The uniform symbolized someone who couldn't be mistreated but also someone he might get rid of at any time. Not that there was anyone he couldn't get rid of—if he wanted to.

And yet, this woman... He was treating her in a way he'd never treated anyone before, even those of much higher status. Status meant nothing to him. Eid had never imagined he would treat someone as if they were the most precious person in the world, as he'd watched Edward do. It was quite refreshing to watch himself act this way, even if it was a dream.

Accepting that this was nothing but a dream and shrugging off how strange it was, Eid watched the dream continue.

But the Eid in the dream began to act like a child. "Stop seeing her."

His tone was unbelievable already, but the woman seemed used to it as she refused to indulge him. "Excuse me? I don't think so."

CHAPTER
FORTY-FIVE

With his unbelievable whining shut down, the Eid in the dream blurted out a cliché recognizable in all cultures.

"Is it her or me?"

Eid immediately covered his face with his hands. He couldn't bear to keep watching. Even if this were a dream, it would be unacceptable. Even the lovestruck Edward wouldn't do something so embarrassing. He found himself suffering from secondhand embarrassment, especially because—as unbelievable as it was—seeing himself this way made it plausible that he could act like this.

Writhing in pain at the embarrassment of it all, he watched the woman let out an exasperated laugh.

"What kind of question is that?" she snorted. *"You know who I would choose."*

For a moment, he was sure she would choose him. He was the emperor, and no one had ever rejected him before, even though he had rejected many. This arrogance and confidence were understandable. He was the mighty emperor.

Dream Eid agreed. He nodded, his expression arrogant. "Yes, of course you would choose m—"

"Of course, I would choose... She'll be my friend forever."

Dream Eid grabbed the back of his neck in shock. So did the real Eid.

At that moment, Eid realized that the Eid in his dream was real. They had the exact same reaction with the exact same pose.

"And me? What about me?"

"I'm not sure."

"Sistina Illid!"

She burst out laughing at his voice, which would have frightened anyone else. Her laugh was brighter than anything. She was like light itself, the warmest and most beautiful light, evident even in a dream.

He thought he might go blind. He thought his eyes would tear up, even though he hadn't cried in years.

It was then that he realized something. He was jealous of the Eid in the dream, the Eid who'd stolen the heart of the woman in this warm scene. He himself was living in the frigid cold, devoid of any warmth, and yet this man was living a completely different life.

This scene, this dream, was beyond what he had ever imagined possible. It was the kind of life he'd given up hoping for a long time ago. It was so warm that it was almost too much for his frozen heart.

"Ugh." Suddenly, his head felt like it was splitting in two. It was the same ache that had been bothering him lately, much more painful this time.

"Sis...tina..."

Amid the haze of pain, a name he hadn't intended to say slipped out. It was like a spark. As soon as he uttered it, his heart began to ache, and breathing became difficult. Tears streamed down his face, dampening his cheeks.

"Sistina... Sina... Sina..."

He crumpled to the ground, murmuring a name he didn't recall ever saying, yet it felt as though he'd uttered it countless times. Strength had fled his legs. He had never felt so powerless, as if all the strength were being sapped from his body. It was as though the gravity of the entire world was pressing down on him, rendering it impossible to rise.

The only thing he could do was call that name. He could do anything for the person who could save him.

Please. I'm begging you. Save me.

"Sina... Sistina..."

As if in answer to his desperate calls, a woman appeared before him. She was like the light.

As soon as she touched him, the weight was lifted, but his heart ached even more. It thumped wildly. Though her touch and warmth were unfamiliar, they felt astonishingly familiar at the same time.

It was then that he suddenly realized something. He knew this woman.

Once again, his head felt like it would split open. His memory turned hazy again, and his lips parted instinctively. "Sistina..."

As if that was the name of the woman before him, the name he remembered.

He could sense that the woman—the woman he couldn't quite see—was smiling. She gently cupped his face in her hands and pressed her lips against his.

Eid felt like crying out in pure joy at her stunning warmth, even though he didn't even know her.

What took you so long? Where have you been?

His whole body rejoiced and welcomed her, even as the excruciating pain worked to erase these feelings.

The woman, as if aware of what was happening, gently caressed his cheeks and whispered, "Eid."

"Sina... Sistina..."

"It's all right."

What is?

"You don't have to remember." She sounded as though she was about to cry.

He couldn't ask her why. The pain was erasing everything too quickly. He wanted to scream, to cry, "No, *stop erasing my memory!*"

But the world had never been on his side.

And so, the light was out.

"No!"

He was chased out of his own dream. Once again, he was left alone.

In a world without her.

"Aaaargh!"

"What in the world—Your Imperial Majesty!"

"Your Imperial Majesty, please calm down. Sire!"

"The physician, call the physician. Hurry!"

"You mustn't, sire."

"Get a hold of yourself, sire."

He couldn't come back, not amid the stream of people crowding around him and Ace's desperate calls. He wanted to cry. He wanted to scream. Without any idea as to why or for what, even though he had no memory of the dream.

"Aaaargh."

But his heart remembered what he had lost.

"Sire!"

The place he belonged.

"I suppose I ought to serve you something, since you're a customer." Shea placed a cup of tea in front of him. It was his favorite, Darjeeling.

Cedric chuckled to himself. She hadn't changed at all. She was still kind, even though she acted like she wasn't, like when he'd arrived here with the child. His heart ached. "Where's the boy?"

"It'd be best for you not to see him."

"I guess so." She was right. He knew he wouldn't be able to restrain his anger, especially if the boy was lovable. "Does he take after Sina?"

"Blood is thicker than water. I tried not to raise him that way, but there was no changing him."

"Pfft. You also failed to change Sina back then."

"Exactly. I suppose I'm no good at raising kids." She wished she'd been better at it.

Cedric smiled faintly at the self-deprecation in her voice. She hadn't changed. "Did you know I would come, Shea?"

"Kind of. Humans don't change easily, and you were always a good kid."

"A kid? Technically, I'm much older than you."

"You would know if you met *him*. Age doesn't mean much to us." She added that she doubted he was here for such silly arguments.

Cedric let out a small sigh at her firm tone. "It's nothing serious. I just—"

"You wanted to see for yourself. And you hoped it would make you feel less guilty."

"..."

She'd hit the nail on the head.

Shea gave him a small smile as he sat there, unable to respond. "I'm not criticizing you. It's because you're a good kid. And a little cowardly."

"That makes no sense."

"Humans don't make sense to begin with."

Cedric held up his hands in defeat. It was a casual and familiar gesture. "I can never beat you in an argument."

Shea picked up her own cup of tea. He hadn't changed at all, either. "So why are you here?"

Cedric let down his carefree façade. "I wanted to hear your final answer."

His fallen, desperate self, which was twisted beyond recognition. *Sistina Illid*, she thought. *You ruined so many people. You should have listened to me. Who told you to leave like that?* "Verdel must have told you already."

"Still."

"Dream on. There is no way in heaven or hell that I would help you."

"..."

She shattered Cedric's hopes in one fell swoop. He gave her another pleading look, but she was immovable. "Is it because of Eid Roux Vencroft?"

"..."

"Do you pity him as well?" he asked.

She burst out laughing, making her answer obvious. "Aren't you the one who actually feels like that toward him? And you're asking me? How ridiculous."

"Shea."

"All right. If you want the full answer, I'll tell you. Yes, I do pity him. Everyone who knows the truth feels the same way."

"I suppose so."

"Even my siblings, who are the most heartless creatures in the world, agree," she said. "I suppose I'm not as heartless as they are."

But whoever knew the truth could only feel sorry for him. Eid Roux Vencroft had everything in the world. Yet although he had so much, none of it was really his. The fact that he'd lost the one thing he held dear could only be pitied, and the way he'd lost it had been so cruel.

"Even you, filled with so much rage, even though he was the reason you lost her," she added, "you still can't blame him for it."

"No, Shea. That's not true."

"..."

"I do blame him. Dozens, maybe hundreds of times a day. If it hadn't been for him, she wouldn't have died. That much is true, isn't it?"

"I suppose so."

It was undeniable. If she hadn't met him to begin with, if she hadn't fallen in love with him, she wouldn't have disappeared from the world so easily.

"That's why I despise him," she said. "I blame him. It's his fault. If only he didn't exist. But I can't keep blaming him. Because I found out something I shouldn't have."

He would have preferred not to know, so he could keep on blaming him.

And Shea felt the same way, so she couldn't say anything.

FORTY-SIX

"You know that he's the unluckiest one," Cedric said. "He lost everything, and yet he can't even remember it. He'll be taken advantage of forever. But maybe that's better than being able to remember? I still don't know, even as I continue to resent him."

"Who knows whether it's a curse or a blessing that he can't remember," Shea said. "One thing's certain: Either way, it's freaking shitty."

He let out an exasperated laugh at her calm tone. "Right. That's what makes me want to vomit. Sacrificing one man's despair, cutting his lifespan, sacrificing person after person. Is it really worth all this?"

"..."

"The Vencroft Empire, I mean."

This broken man, whose ardent love had lost its purpose, was laying his heart bare. Shea found herself at a loss. He wouldn't listen to whatever she had to say, and there was always the possibility that she might break him again. She wondered what she could do for this broken man.

"The reason I waited for you today…"

"…"

"…was neither to stop you, nor to comfort you, nor to tell you I would join you.

"…"

 It was to tell you her will."

"Her will?"

Yes, her last words. The last words she said to me right before she disappeared from this world.

"She asked me to give you one chance, for her brother, who would grieve her death. Because her kind brother will regret it."

"Sina."

The mere mention of her shook him. It made Shea wonder how such a weak, sensitive man could do something so drastic. They said that good people who went insane became terrifying. Perhaps this was one of those cases. It made her pity him. He was going to break in the end, and that was not what she'd have wanted. But she knew that this pitiful man wouldn't be able to stop, regardless, so she gave him some heartfelt advice.

"We, including me, won't stop you," she said. "We don't think Vencroft is worth much, either. But that doesn't mean we'll jump on the opportunity and bring about the apocalypse sooner. This is a matter to be settled among humans. It isn't something for us to meddle with."

"..."

"We also have no right to interfere with your choice to vent your grief in this way."

"..."

"However, I don't want you to regret it. In the end, it's your decision to make."

"Shea." Cedric lowered his head. He couldn't look her in the eye. To Cedric, Shea Grande had always been on a pedestal, completely out of reach. He could completely understand why Roux had chosen her. "Thank you, Shea."

She smiled in the genuine gratitude in his words. "I suppose I do feel bad for him. It was something he was protecting—with a sacrifice he hadn't wished for and doesn't even remember."

"Verdel told me that it was strange the emperor hasn't gone on a rampage yet," Cedric said. "There's no way the memory-altering curse wouldn't have run out by now."

"I suppose that makes sense. It may have altered his memory—but if he went through life without remembering anything, it wouldn't be much of a curse. He wouldn't even remember he'd forgotten something."

"That's your doing, isn't it?" Cedric sounded sure of himself. Only Shea could have done something like this. As far as he knew, she was the only one.

She hadn't been trying to keep it a secret—no one had ever asked—so she didn't hesitate to confirm his suspicion. "It was a small gift from me."

Technically, it had been one of *her* last wishes—the last thing that damn girl had told her. *"If he's going to forget, please make sure he forgets forever. Because he'll definitely be sad."*

"Are you seriously worrying about him right now?"

"I loved him."

What is love, anyway? Shea remembered the rage bubbling up inside her as she watched her friend in such a terrible state. She'd wanted her to be angry at him.

"Can't you see that's why you've ended up like this?"

"That's why. It would pain me too much if I ended up like this and he had to suffer as well."

"You—"

"Please, Shea. If not forever, please let him forget for as long as possible."

"You're asking so much of me."

"I'm sorry. I'm sorry, Shea, for ending up like this."

"If you're sorry, you should have avoided this entire situation, you damn girl."

"You're right."

And with a smile, she'd passed away. She'd faded away so helplessly that Shea couldn't ignore her last wish. If she didn't at least do that for her, her death would have been in vain. Although it was something she'd sworn never to do, she'd had no choice.

"It isn't perfect," Shea said. "Enough time has passed, and it will wear off soon."

"Wear off?"

"I'm not sure. Memories tend to come back through dreams, and it will probably be the same for him."

"..."

Whether it was remembering things lost through amnesia or regaining memories of a past life, such things often occurred through dreams, as in many other novels. In the end, people realized that those dreams were memories. She knew this because she'd experienced it herself.

And even though she knew what it felt like, she was curious. "I wonder what he's thinking as he dreams about the past?"

Eid couldn't sleep. He thought he might go insane if he did. He feared having another dream. Having stayed awake for days, he was now in such a state that he dreamed even when he was awake.

This time, it seemed like something that had happened before the last dream, not long after they'd met. She'd been working as a maid, and she was put in charge of cleaning his room, a job none of the servants wanted.

Though he must've been the most fearsome person in the imperial palace, she treated him like any other person. *"Yikes! You look like you're ready to kill someone, Your Imperial Majesty."*

It was astonishing. And that was exactly why a maid intrigued him for the first time.

"You're impudent. You're nothing but a maid."

"I'll find another job if I get fired. My friend was against me working here, anyway. The pay is nice, so that part would be a little sad."

She was impudent and cheeky.

"Aren't you worried that I might kill you?"

"No."

She was fearless, as well.

"Why not?"

The fact that her behavior didn't bother him was astounding. And so, he was slow but surely drawn to her.

"Well, *my friend always tells me that I'm a terrible judge of character, you see. She says a teddy bear would have better insight than me.*"

"*...*"

What a harsh thing to say. He wondered who this friend was because her critiques were so unique and ruthless.

"So, *when I asked why she thought I was so bad at it, she told me this. I only ever see the good in people. And that's nice, but it's also why people always take advantage of me.*"

Though he wasn't sure whether this was supposed to be praise or an insult, judging by the naive look on her face, he decided that this analysis was very much true. As if to prove her friend's point, she was far too relaxed in front of him. She really should have been running away. She certainly was a bad judge of character.

As if blissfully unaware of what he was thinking, she gave him her usual innocent smile and continued. "So, to me, you do seem like a person to be feared, but not someone who would kill anyone so easily. And I have a feeling I won't die in your hands."

Her bluntness was amazing. He found himself enthralled, whether by her smile or her words.

"Liar," *he croaked.* You said you wouldn't die. You said you'd stay with me forever.

"Your Imperial Majesty?"

"Medicine…"

"Pardon?"

"Get me my pills at once."

"Y-yes, sire."

The waking world greeted with excruciating pain. It felt as though it would be a relief to rip out his heart. Eid gritted his teeth as he endured pain enough to make him feel faint. His memory was already growing hazy again.

He had to remember.

He couldn't forget again.

"Sire, I've brought your medicine."

"Mmph."

Ace stared in awe as Eid downed the incredibly bitter medicine like it was nothing. He wondered whether the emperor had lost his sense of taste as well. Then he realized something, as violent sobs erupted from Eid's throat: The time was near. The hour of his fate.

Ace had been ready for it for a long time.

He was ready to meet his death. He had been ready to pay for his sin with his life, ever since that day long ago.

By the time Shea saw Cedric off, the sun had already set, so she decided to give up on delivering her bribe today and turned back to get started tidying up.

"Shea!" It was a voice she'd been missing, even though she'd pretended not to.

"Why did you come so late?" She took an angry tone on purpose to try and mask her feelings, but it didn't seem to work.

Edward's smile was brighter than ever. "I missed you, Shea." He ran to her like the wind and squeezed her tightly, professing over and over how much he'd missed her.

"Ugh, you're crushing me."

"I missed you."

His desperate voice tugged at her heartstrings. *As always, you are honest, and I know you so well. You loved me over and over like this.* "I missed you too."

So much so that you make me want to come up with excuses to do things I would never otherwise do, just to see you. It had been an excuse, saying that she was planning to do something bad and bribe someone. All of it was an excuse to go and see him.

It wasn't as if she'd ever cared about good or bad. She'd never been that ethical, and she certainly didn't care about morals.

A bribe? Yeah, right.

It was yet another secret to add to the pile. But because she was already keeping so many, it hardly mattered.

CHAPTER
FORTY-SEVEN

It wasn't much of a secret, more like something she'd rather not reveal. Not a secret. Just something that wouldn't do anyone any good to know.

She didn't care if that meant she was being deceitful. He didn't need to know. She'd already decided to take the responsibility herself.

"Let's go inside."

As they entered the café, Edward tilted his head in confusion. The usual warmth he felt when he entered the café wasn't there today. "Where are the others?"

"Oh, I sent them to Grande."

"Oh? Why?"

For a moment, she doubted his intelligence. "The situation here isn't great. It's much safer in Grande than the capital." Though the capital was in turmoil, Grande was fine. It was entirely independent—so unlike the capital, which was affected by every little change in the empire. Grande wasn't easily shaken. "Grande is a thousand times better for a child than the capital."

"That's true."

"And Fel is still here."

"Fel?"

She blinked at him, wondering why he didn't know Fel, but then she remembered. Fel kept a low profile so that the regulars at Sangria, many of whom worked at the imperial palace, wouldn't recognize him as a former imperial knight captain. It wasn't a tactic that worked on Shea, who sensed people by their souls rather than their presence. But since none of the nobles or ministers who frequented Sangria had recognized him over the years, she'd forgotten about his former status.

"Oh, I forgot," she said. "Never mind."

"What is it? Who is he?"

"Stop overthinking it. He's one of my servants, easy to overlook. That's why you don't know him."

"That's it?"

That wasn't all there was to it, of course, but she decided not to elaborate. He didn't need to know. "Stop imagining things. He's married, you know."

He was only married in his heart—but still. She thought it was a perfectly justifiable statement, and it wasn't entirely untrue, so there was no issue. The man had an unchanging iron will.

"Oh, sorry."

Nice. Got him. As previously mentioned, Shea had no morals, and so she decided to use this opportunity. "Sorry? Is that all?"

Edward tried to bribe her with material goods, a tactic that worked on most people. "Hmm... is there anything you would like?"

But unfortunately...

"Wow, look at you trying to use money to get out of a rough patch. What am I going to do with this insincere attitude of yours?"

...Shea was immune to such things.

I have far too much money to begin with. Not that she'd earned most of it herself. Her underlings had done all the work. But although she wasn't as rich as the highest-ranking nobles, she wasn't greedy, either. She had more than enough to live comfortably, without ever having to work.

Though she'd only teased him a bit, Edward already seemed close to his limit. "D-do you want me to cook for you?"

"What?"

What? Did you say you would cook? For me? Someone who makes the best food in this world, who could easily get three Michelin stars?

She wasn't exactly exasperated, but rather surprised and impressed by his bravery in even offering to cook for her. No one had ever proposed such a thing in her entire life, not even her mother and father in this world.

"You're far better at it, so why don't you cook for us?"

Shea had always been in charge of cooking. To be fair, her mother had been hopeless at it, so Shea never complained. She didn't want to starve. Thankfully, she'd been raised on food made by a hired helper her father worked extra hard to afford, convincing his wife with his charm by telling her that he didn't want her to work so hard when Shea was young.

"I-is that a no?"

"Are you any good at cooking?"

"I'll try my best!"

She found herself smiling at the sight of Edward refusing to take back his offer, even as he began to sweat. How could she not smile? He always tried his best, steeling his resolve over and over again so that he could stay true to his word. It was so lovable. "I'll practice my acting, then."

She sat down and watched as Edward entered the kitchen and awkwardly began to take out pots and pans.

Clink. Clatter.

She rested her chin on her hand and smiled.

"Are you... going to sit there and watch?" he asked.

"I'll scold you if you do anything wrong."

"Pfft. All right."

Though he looked unpracticed—which was no surprise—the sight of him trying his best to cook for her made her inexplicably happy. Happiness wasn't that difficult to find. Something so seemingly trivial was enough. But maybe that was why it was more difficult and more prominent in its absence.

Love wasn't much different. She'd never hoped for a grand love story, like in the movies. All she'd hoped for were small, seemingly insignificant moments that were all the more meaningful.

Small but lovely moments like this.

"Add the onions now."

"All right."

Hiss.

Without this, she felt empty. Her heart lost its purpose. And she'd never been able to get used to that emptiness. She'd cried so much.

She hated love.

But even as she regretted it—even as she tutted at the sight of other couples who didn't have a happy ending, who had loved each other but ended up miserable—she had never claimed they shouldn't have loved in the first place. Because she knew. As painful as it was...

"Shea! It's done."

"Ooh, that actually looks good."

"Could you say something that sounds like an actual compliment, please?"

"*Haha.* I'll have to try it first."

...she knew that she would keep going for days like these. *Because* of days like these. *So as hopeless, insane, and idiotic as it may be, I will keep on loving you...*

"It's good!" she exclaimed. "This isn't your first time, is it?"

"I made soup when I was in the military and camping."

"It's great. Well done, boyfriend."

"Thank you, girlfriend."

...and find happiness.

Eid felt like he had gone insane.

"*Wow, really?*"

"*I'm telling you... and... were...*"

"*No way! And what happened then?*"

He was watching a dream, even though he was awake. Even though that was clearly impossible.

Is this *magic?* Someone must've cast magic on him, to make him see things. That did seem more plausible than going insane or dreaming while awake. If this were the case, he swore to kill whoever had done this to him—and their death would not be quick. This went beyond mischief. It was catastrophic. At this point...

"Eid!"

"Stop running. You'll trip and fall."

"I'm f—ahhh!"

"Sistina!"

...seeing these scenes was making him go insane. He couldn't function normally. It was impossible. Just the sight of her made his heart ache and his head go blank.

"Sire?"

As he returned to reality at the sound of Ace's voice, Eid scoffed at the overwhelming sense of emptiness, now that the pain had subsided.

Then something occurred to him, something he thought he'd gotten over a long time ago. Something he hadn't expected to ever affect him because it had already run its course. Something crucial in Vencroft's history.

"I suppose it's finally gotten to me," he said.

"Pardon?"

The Vencroft curse. No one had been able to avoid it, and he was no exception. He never imagined how it might manifest. At most, he thought it would come to him as a sort of bloodlust.

How foolish he had been. Of course, the notorious curse wouldn't be something so trivial. He understood now why every single one of them had gone mad. It was inevitable.

Every vision pierced his heart.

His forbears must have experienced something similar. His father had gone insane and died at his own hands. Eid had looked down on his father then and thought him pathetic. How foolish of him.

His father's last words had sounded like a curse. *"Do not fool yourself. You will not be any different!"*

Eid always wondered why those words stayed with him. Now he realized that they were meant for this day. Back then, he'd thought of his father's outburst as the petulant words of a dying man, but the sentiment must have come from experience.

He recalled something else, as well. His father hadn't been as insane as the others, and he'd tried his best to be a good father. The madness was what changed him in the end.

Is that what will happen to me?

"Ace."

"Yes, sire."

He closed his eyes, his voice calm. "What is the average time between the Vencroft curse first showing itself and the final descent into insanity?"

Ace's heart dropped. The Vencroft curse. The mere mention was enough to make his heart sink, but having it brought up by a victim made it all the more impactful. "Pardon? Why, all of a sudden—"

"Answer."

Ace's mind went blank. Though he'd always thought himself brilliant, his brain turned to stone, unwilling to function. *Why? For what reason?*

"There was a lot of variation according to the symptoms," he replied slowly, "but on average, it takes about two years."

"I see." It was quite a bit of time. Eid had genuinely expected less. Though two years was a ridiculously short amount of time in one sense, it was also enough time to get things done. "How many members of the imperial family are left, Ace?"

"Just one."

"Excluding me."

"None."

CHAPTER
FORTY-EIGHT

They had all killed each other and died at each other's hands. Since Eid had participated in the killing himself, he knew very well that he was the only one of the Vencrofts left.

He sighed. It was true. He had ascended to the throne precisely because the rest of the family had slaughtered each other, and then he himself had killed his father.

"What about a distant cousin or someone who could take the throne?"

"Have you finally decided to have a child or something?"

Eid frowned at Ace's cheeky way of saying that no, there was no one else. "So, when I die, it will be the end of Vencroft for good."

"Isn't that what you hoped for?"

"I did. I hoped for it so much that, if I knew it would help, I would have lived my life as a devout follower of the Great God Roux."

"…"

Ace was left speechless by the spite in Eid's voice. It reminded him of someone... someone who had influenced Eid, making him sound so cynical.

Eid sounded almost fiercely sharp. "But I'm certain you never hoped for this empire to fall."

"..."

No, I... Ace couldn't bring himself to say it. *Never.* Not to the man in front of him. He didn't have the courage to add to his already endless heap of hypocrisy.

"So, look for someone who might be able to take the throne after me."

"If it is not someone from the Vencroft bloodline," Ace said, "the god's blessing will end. Though it may be superstition, please remember that many believe in it."

No one would acknowledge anyone but a member of the Vencroft family as a successor.

Eid clucked his tongue in annoyance. "Haven't they had enough? It's been long enough."

"..."

Humans had always been shameless. As a species, they perpetually wanted more and felt entitled to additional favors far too easily. It never seemed to occur to them that those favors might someday come to an end.

"They have no other choice," Eid added.

"..."

"Even if not for the curse, I will be gone someday."

The curse will not come to you, because you are already cursed. Ace couldn't voice the words on the tip of his tongue. It was cowardly and pathetic, the way he acted.

Eid ignored Ace's inner turmoil. Looking noble, as befitting of someone with imperial blood, he commanded, "Find the next best alternative."

To prepare for my inevitable death.

After taking care of some paperwork, Eid trudged down the hallway in a daze. He wasn't sure he was heading in the right direction because he was still hearing voices in his head.

"I love you."

"I'm serious, you know!"

"I love you."

"Really?"

"Really."

His own ecstatic voice. Her joyful laughter at the sound of his voice.

He felt like he couldn't breathe.

It was nothing new. The ache in his chest was normal now, and he continued to feel like he was dying. If someone told him to die right here, right now, he thought he wouldn't mind. If he could just die.

The reason he didn't pull out his sword and end it himself was because he had a feeling that wouldn't be enough to kill him. Realistically, even if he stabbed himself, too many people would rush in to keep him alive. His skillful subordinates would have no problem succeeding. Though he would suffer from the wounds, he would continue to live.

And that was worse.

But he was strangely convinced he wouldn't be able to die anyway. It wasn't his time yet. It was a gut feeling.

Thinking about it made him feel even more depressed.

Am I supposed to keep watching these scenes? Continuously? While enduring this pain? For what reason?

Dying would be much better. He wasn't particularly attached to his life, anyway. It was everyone else who didn't want him to die. Not that it would do them any good.

"Eid! Eid!"

"Why are you here?"

"Perhaps it's punishment."

He wondered whether this was punishment for living the way he had. He closed his eyes, numb. This was the most he could do so he wouldn't despair.

He didn't want to keep watching.

He didn't want to keep despairing.

He didn't want to blame the tears that no longer flowed.

Who in the world are you? Why are you doing this to me?

The questions kept coming, even though he knew no one would answer them.

He wished she would appear before him. He wanted her to appear so he could blame her or do whatever he needed to. He wanted it so desperately that he was ready to beg on his knees, anyone, even his worst enemy.

But he knew very well that this wish couldn't be fulfilled. He knew instinctively that he would never be able to meet her.

Damn it.

"I wish I was a fool."

He didn't want to know the reality of it all. He wished he could hope for an impossible dream, like a fool.

"I'm not cold ye—"

"Stop lying!"

"You barely ever get cold, either."

"Are you comparing yourself to me?"

"If you were to exist..."

Though he didn't remember her face or her name, he knew that he would fall in love with her if she stood before him now. For some reason, he didn't doubt it.

He was certain. Certain that he would do things even crazier than Edward, who'd gone completely insane with love. He would get on his knees to greet her if she suddenly appeared before him.

"Damn it."

He felt like crying, but he had no more tears to shed. Unending despair clouded his vision. It was as though he was staring at a white wall. He didn't know where or how to go.

He placed his hands over his eyes in despair. This wasn't going to achieve anything, but he couldn't stop.

Damn it.

He wished he could die so he wouldn't be able to see these visions anymore. So that he wouldn't have to face such despair.

So that I can meet you. The thought made him flinch in surprise, and he remembered this was a dream he had once, rather than a memory.

"She told me to be wary of handsome men."

He'd been so exasperated.

The Eid in the dream had been so flabbergasted by the strange statement, which was beyond anything he could have ever come up with himself. He had cried out to her, *"Who in the world told you that?"*

And she answered. *"Shea did. Was she wrong?"*

"...!"

That's what she said. She spoke the name "Shea." Though the name wasn't common, there were probably countless women named Shea in the empire.

But only one person came to Eid's mind.

"Shea Grande." He turned on his heel and began to sprint.

He had to see her. No matter what.

Meanwhile, Sangria was as busy as always.

"Shea!"

"Why did you send Lucy away?"

"That's none of your business," Shea replied.

"Then at least make up for the work she does."

"That's none of your business, either."

"Are you running a café or not?"

"Didn't you know? I only opened it because you begged, even though I told you to leave."

Sniff.

Oh, he's crying. Wow. She stared into space to ignore the sight of a grown man sobbing.

Everyone despaired when they saw how uninterested she was. They lost their fighting spirit and trudged out the door. *We're doomed. She's in a daze.*

They'd still had a nice day. Though she wasn't friendly in any way and hadn't treated her customers well, the drinks Shea made tasted much better than those made by Lucy. Shea really was the best. They would return tomorrow because of it.

"See you again." Shea dryly said goodbye to her customers without any sincerity, completely unaware of—or ignoring—their feelings. *Don't come back, please.* Once they'd left and the café was finally empty, she got up and stretched her arms over her head. "They're finally gone."

They always stayed far too long for her liking.

With a few more complaints, she went about tidying up the place for the day, with Fel's help. She grumbled to herself as she swept the floor.

Sangria had always succeeded based on her desserts and Lucy's customer service. As wonderful as Shea's cooking was, her café would never have grown so popular without Lucy. Lucy balanced Shea's lack of respect for her customers. Without Lucy, nobody would want to visit the café, despite her cooking. The place had been even more out of control than usual.

"Shea, Shea—one macaron, please."

"A piece of strawberry tart for me."

"No, lemon meringue pie."

"I want a blueberry cream bun, too."

Without Lucy to serve as a gatekeeper, the customers had overwhelmed Shea. She tried telling them to get out, but it didn't work. In the end, their incessant demands had become so annoying that Shea was forced to work.

She hadn't expected this. "Why do we have to work, anywaaay? I want to eat, sleep, and play all daaay. There is no end to my suffering, and life continues to be haaard."

Even Fel, who had witnessed a lot of things from Shea, looked exasperated as she came up with ridiculous lyrics to a generic melody.

It did sound a lot like her, though.

Tidying up didn't take long, since she hadn't done much cooking today. "Hmm, now I have to turn the sign to Closed and lock the doors."

"Then I'll go upstairs first."

"All right. Good night, Fel." Shea stepped outside the café door. "It must be fall already."

Spring and summer had passed in what seemed like the blink of an eye. It had been a chaotic two seasons—now that she thought about it. So many things had happened. Something she'd given up on had returned. She was doing something insane yet again. And something she'd hoped wouldn't happen was happening.

It really had been a chaotic few months.

CHAPTER
FORTY-NINE

In fact, my entire life has been chaotic, Shea thought. *Why did so many things have to happen? I didn't wish for any of it. Damn it.*

"Come to think of it, it's already been five years since you've been gone." It was already fall again—the season she died in. Soon to be winter... when she was buried.

Then again, I was the one who buried you in the winter.

"Five years already."

It still felt like it had happened not long ago, and yet five years had passed.

Time flew by.

Five years.

Shea assessed the weight of that time. It wasn't a short period. It was enough for anyone to feel that it had been a while.

It was the amount of time she'd bought for him.

I wonder if it was enough for you to be forgotten, enough time for you to fade into nothing but a fond memory. Was it enough time for him to have grown numb to your loss, even if he does remember?

The time she bought for him wouldn't last forever. People's memories and feelings couldn't be buried for long. She didn't want to keep them buried. But it had lasted a lot longer than she'd expected, though she didn't know whether it was because *she* was easy to forget or the opposite. Either way, there was nothing she could do now.

There was no way to turn back time.

"Ugh, I should get some sleep." She shook her head a few times to rid herself of those thoughts and turned to go back inside.

"Shea Grande!"

"...!"

She turned reflexively to the desperate, anguished cry. And there he was—the man she had always expected.

"Eid Roux Vencroft."

She'd thought about it a lot—about how she was going to face him if he remembered everything. And yet, despite years of contemplating it, faced with this man, who looked so desperate...

"You know about Sina—Sistina, don't you?" he demanded.

"..."

...she still wasn't sure what to say to him.

"You know about her, right? About Sina."

"..."

She found herself at a loss for words. She watched him stand there, looking as though he might crumple to the ground at any moment. On the one hand, the fact that this man was standing in front of her comforted her, because it meant that *she* had really been loved. But seeing him so broken, she wanted to blame him, to pity him, to tell him he should've been better or worse so that this never would have happened.

She figured that Cedric, who was doing something completely insane, probably felt the same way, which was why he hadn't been able to dispose of Eid. Even though it would have been so much simpler to kill one man.

Shea had felt the same way for a long time, and so she found herself in a dilemma. She wondered whether this man, who would otherwise never have been so affected and who was so broken without even knowing the whole story, could now bear the whole truth. In the end, it hadn't been his fault.

The foolish Eid, who had no idea she was sympathizing with him, grew agitated by her silence.

"Shea!"

Only then did Shea emerge from her reverie. "Why do you think I know her?"

Is she feigning ignorance?

But Shea's expression was completely composed, as if she were making sure.

Her calm was almost infectious, but he couldn't quite catch it. Confusion had overtaken his mind. "Sina. Sina said so. She said your name. I'm sure of it!"

He sounded almost like a child. His reasoning was weak. But Shea couldn't find it in her to look down on Eid. She couldn't make fun of him, either, though she wished she could.

"Eid Roux Vencroft."

"Stop denying it. I know you know her, so tell me. Everything! This is an order!" Though he looked ready to burst into tears, his words were pompous.

Shea felt like ridiculing him for it. Her mood was ruined. "Hey."

"Are you going to tell me?" He looked ready to sink into the ground now.

The sight of him made her blood boil.

Damn it, Sistina Illid. You were always too damn naive to judge anyone's character properly, but your eye for men was even worse. Why did you choose someone like him?

"I ask you, Eid Roux Vencroft: If I were to tell you the truth, would you be able to handle it?"

"...!"

"How do you so easily ask for an answer when you don't even have the slightest idea what my answer might be?"

It was exasperating. Judging by the way he was acting, her seal was certainly wearing off, but it hadn't worn off completely yet. That probably meant that he himself was keeping it going. The seal she'd placed on him hadn't been very strong to begin with. Too much time would only make the pain fester and turn into something worse.

And so, this ticked her off. He was demanding the truth from her as if he were entitled to it, even though he was giving power to the seal that blocked his memory. He wasn't ready for the truth whatsoever.

"Whatever truth you're looking for, you don't appear to be ready. I'm not a nice enough person to waste my time explaining every single thing to someone who hasn't even regained his memory."

"..."

"So, if you want me to tell you anything, go and retrieve your own memory first." It would be the right thing to do, out of respect for the love he'd lost and the woman who'd loved him. *Once you remember everything, I'll reveal even the truths you don't know.*

"I told her I loved her. I begged her to stay, but..." Eid mumbled in a daze, as if he'd begun to remember something.

She turned her back on him and went back inside the café, Smart enough to know that hesitation would only make the situation worse.

Creak... Clack.

As soon as she locked the door behind her, a flash of awareness went through her head. She didn't know how to react. "It feels like this time... it's the topaz of the West. Cedric must be serious about this."

There wasn't much time left until this thousand-year-long movie would come to an end.

"A report from the West! The guardian cannot be located, and a sudden heat wave is causing the crops to dry up and die."

"What?"

It was an empire-wide emergency.

Even though the North had gone to ruin after the northern guardian stone had been destroyed, the report about the West was received very differently.

"Good heavens!"

"Wh-what about food reserves? Has anything been harvested already?"

"Apparently the flu has been going around in the West, so the harvest has been pushed back. Only the most hardworking farmers typically started so early, so they hadn't begun yet."

Nothing had been harvested. Everyone rose up in anger that not a single crop could be saved.

"What do you mean, nothing?"

"The West is the empire's breadbasket. Why weren't they more cautious?"

"Who's in charge of the region? Throw that scumbag in jail!"

"You mean you haven't thrown him in jail yet?"

It was utter chaos.

There was no better way to describe it, thought the youngest member of the department, who had made the report. He watched on, feeling helpless.

Their reaction wasn't unwarranted. The report he had made was so obviously serious that it would have made even a clueless child cry. Even a child would know that a lack of food was bad.

"We need a plan, now. Use your brains—every last brain cell!"

"Before you do that, use your hands. Find out how much was rationed. Last year's harvest was plentiful, so there should be a lot left, right?"

"The mages—ask the mages. Tell them to hurry and check whether any crops can be saved."

"Come up with emergency crops first, unless you want to eat nothing but dirt next year."

The fact that another ward had been broken was a huge issue in and of itself. The even bigger issue was that over two-thirds of the empire's crops were grown in the West, due to its mild climate. The empire was blessed with soil across the land that was good for growing crops, but the West, with its rich soil and expansive fields, had become the empire's breadbasket. Growing high-quality crops there was as easy as throwing seeds over the ground, and the yield had always been so large that there was always more than enough to export to the rest of the empire. There had never been a need for the other regions to grow more.

The other regions now relied on the West for their crops. There wasn't the need for other regions to go through the hard work of farming when they could get anything they needed from the West.

But the ruination of the West's crops meant ruin for the whole empire.

The empire was wealthy, but food was a different matter. People couldn't eat money. It was obvious what would happen if the empire were forced to import food from other nations, thereby making its food shortage known.

It was a total disaster.

"Sir Yuri, we've received a reply from the mage tower. They say no magic can bring back those crops."

"How dare they! What kind of bastard sends back a reply like that?"

"Sir Yuri, they say there was far too much harvest to store and maintain by magic, so it was all exported to the desert. There are currently only three warehouses' worth of extra rations."

"What scumbag is responsible for this?"

"Shall we imprison them?"

"What kind of question is that? Throw them out the window."

The administration department was in complete chaos.

CHAPTER
FIFTY

Documents went flying everywhere, leaving hardly any room to walk on the floor, so people stepped on the papers. Everyone was starting to lose their minds. New problems continued to pop up, while none were being resolved. The only reason they were still standing was because they knew that fainting would achieve absolutely nothing.

The head of the administrative department, Yuri Menthier, desperately held onto his sanity. "What do we even have? We must do something to stop people from rioting."

Riots weren't the only problem. At this point, the empire was headed for ruin. For the citizens of an empire that had lived in prosperity for hundreds of years, going hungry was unimaginable.

"The only unaffected fields in the West are those managed by Sir Byron," said one employee.

"...!"

Everyone's eyes widened at the mention of the unspeakable name.

Byron.

There wasn't a single person at the imperial palace, especially in the administrative department, who hadn't heard his name. It was the first thing they were taught: the story of how the Children of God, the representatives of the Great God Roux, hated the temple so much that they hid their identities so that not a single one of them could be found. None had ever been captured by the temple against their will.

However, there was one individual, a Child of God, who had never gone into hiding. He was living in the West, tending to his farm. He was the only Child of God that the temple knew about: the Child of Peace, Dean Byron.

As his title indicated, he valued peace above all else. He'd managed to live his life without interference, and anyone who threatened his way of life was disposed of without hesitation. This meant that despite his location being known, no one could use or even approach him.

Yuri wanted to go ahead and faint, the empire be damned.

"Ugh, are you kidding me?"

The news spread almost instantly.

"The West?"

"No way."

"What's going to happen to us, then?"

"What else? We're going to die."

All the crops in the West had suddenly died.

Those who knew what this meant turned pale with dread. Those who had already been anxious over what happened in the North began to panic as well. They would be out of food, and all the money in the world wouldn't help.

"Wheat—give me everything you have."

"Everything?"

"Yes."

"B-but you can't—"

"Who do you think I am? Sell it to me this instant!"

Despite their duty to mitigate the mass hysteria, the nobles began to panic-buy wheat, driving up the price.

"What? How much? Are you kidding me?"

"Get out if you're not buying. You shouldn't even be touching it if you can't afford it."

"What did you say?"

It was so bad that wheat, which had always been cheap and affordable even for the lower classes, went from one silver per sack to at least three gold.

Meanwhile, the temple continued to claim that this was happening because the people had stopped worshipping Roux and that he was enraged. A Child of God had returned to the temple, which they cited as a reason for people to join them.

This made life at the imperial palace even more difficult. More outrageous still was the fact that increasing numbers of people were joining the temple. Many, having enjoyed the comforts of the empire's golden age, sought something to rely on at the first sign of trouble. The return of a true Child of God to the temple made their joining almost inevitable.

The nobles were no exception. Instead of banding together to get through this, it was every man for himself. It was human nature. Everyone valued themselves more than anyone or anything else.

And so, even those who criticized the temple for splitting the nation found themselves seeking the temple's help—or rather, the help of the Child of God residing in it.

They went to see Verdel and asked him to save them. They asked if the Children of God, those blessed with powers by Roux, would rise up to save everyone. They asked, even though they knew how the empire had been built and that the Children of God had never sworn to protect it.

They wanted to be saved.

Verdel only smiled at them.

That was all, but it was enough. Nobody was foolish enough not to recognize the cold indifference behind that smile. It dug deep into their hearts as it sliced through their shameful selfishness. In the end, they couldn't blame him or plead with him. None of them could argue or ask how he could be so heartless, because his presence showed them how unworthy they were.

The imperial palace was everyone's last resort. The people pleaded with the palace, writing countless letters asking them to please do something. The administrative department was overwhelmed even further, on top of the other departments that had already ceased to function.

"Duke Morgan now owns sixty percent of the available wheat."

"Ugh, we're swamped. Why does he have to start hoarding now?"

"Duke Maxwell won't miss this chance."

"This *chance*? Really? Come on."

Even as the imperial palace struggled to secure as much wheat as possible, the dukes hoarded resources to try and gain more power.

Yuri pulled out his own hair. He was already going bald, but he needed something to hold onto to keep his sanity. He needed to keep believing that the empire wasn't going to go to ruin soon.

Not that it even mattered.

"Sir Yuri, stop pulling your hair. Here—a message from Sir Griffith."

"What are you waiting for? What does it say?"

"It just arrived. He reports that the South should be able to sustain itself. Many people have their own fields and grow their own food, so they should be able to make do without wheat from the West."

"That's good news. Be vigilant. If you're not careful with that information, people might start flocking to the South *en masse* and ruin everything."

"Understood."

"He can't have gone home yet. I'm amazed he already found out this information. He must be as amazing as ever."

"He's the exception. Though I don't remember the last time we got to go home."

"When was the last time I went home? It's been at least a week."

Yuri looked forlorn and sighed.

The official gazed into the distance and muttered to himself, "How are we supposed to go home when the emperor himself made sure we had bathrooms and bedrooms right next door?"

"Right?"

It had been much more intimidating than telling them to stay. Without so much as a word, the emperor had provided rooms for every single official in administration, complete with bathrooms, maids, and physicians for anyone who got sick. Though it was kind of him to provide such things, it didn't escape any of them that this was a form of wordless coercion.

That was even scarier.

Just use your words. Just tell us that we'll never get to go home.

"It's not only us, though."

"True."

The only comfort was that they weren't the only ones suffering. The Ministries of Defense, Finance, and International Relations were working to death, as well. Everyone accepted this reality in their own ways.

Yuri thought this was even scarier. And the fact that the emperor had such power over every department was equally terrifying.

"Anyway, keep an eye on Duke Maxwell. And regarding the North, ignore them for now, but keep an eye on the East. You have someone spying on the temple?"

"Of course. They seem to be ecstatic with their new followers. They're proselytizing to the entire countryside by bringing them wheat."

"So, they have more than enough money."

"They can always leech off everyone."

Yuri responded with an annoyed cluck of his tongue. "All that's left is the East and the South. Who in the world is responsible for this madness, anyway?"

"It might be the temple."

"No, even the temple seems surprised by this. It makes them nervous, but they're using this opportunity to lure people in. They're crazy—not that they weren't before."

It seemed as though the priests had given up on being human. With this cynical assessment of the temple, Yuri picked up one of the many documents piled on his desk. "In any case, the culprits have no intention of stopping, if they've gone this far. The military is in charge of capturing them, so we'll leave it to them. We need to keep thinking of countermeasures in case things keep getting worse."

The official, who knew what he had to do next but was overcome with anxiety, spoke up with a trembling voice. "What happens if they all disappear?"

Yuri spoke the cold, hard truth in a cynical, unwavering tone. "What else? We become like everyone else. Like all the other nations that regularly suffer from droughts, floods, and monster invasions."

"Wow, what an absolute mess." Shea, who hadn't been to the market in a while, found herself genuinely impressed by the chaotic scene before her. The markets were always a bit chaotic, bustling with activity, but this was beyond that. "These prices are outrageous! Are you kidding me?"

"If you aren't buying, go away. Stop wasting my time."

She glared right back. "How could you charge one gold per basket? This is robbery!"

"What?"

It was absolute chaos.

CHAPTER
FIFTY-ONE

It wasn't just one shop but the whole market, making the place feel like a back alley with its swearing and aggression. It was almost shocking that a fistfight hadn't broken out yet and people hadn't started looting shops.

Shea found herself impressed by the citizens of the empire. *I guess people have enough common sense.* In cases of mass hysteria, it was normal for people to loot shops and hurt each other like a pack of rabid beasts. There were countless examples of this in human history.

This was one bad harvest, but for the citizens of Vencroft, it must have been a huge shock. Their lives had been easy, and this sudden, unexpected hardship must feel like the end of the world to them. Shea wouldn't have been surprised if the empire fell as soon as the guardian stone of the West, the topaz, was destroyed—that's how little she expected from the people of the empire. But now that she had seen the state of the market, she readjusted her expectations.

It could've been much worse.

Fel stared at the scene, dumbstruck. "What are you going to buy?"

"I was going to buy some meat and vegetables, but... do you want to go into that chaos, Fel?"

Fel's answer was immediate. "Let's go back home." He left no room for argument.

Shea shrugged and turned away. "Man, I really wanted steak tonight."

Fel stopped in his tracks. He was a sucker for Shea's steaks, eating five extra-large portions at a time, despite Shea's act that cooking so much was bothersome. He looked back and forth between Shea and the market, conflicted, before steeling his resolve and following Shea. As much as he loved steak, he didn't love food *that* much.

Shea let out a small chuckle, as if she knew exactly what was going on in his head. But she didn't do anything in response, which was very like her. If anyone else saw someone in such a dilemma, they might consider going in to buy meat themselves, but that wasn't the case for Shea. It was Fel's own problem to deal with. It was quite inconsiderate of her.

But Fel didn't seem to be bothered by her reaction, as if he expected her to act this way.

Shea found it strange that he so easily accepted her for who she was and let out another chuckle. She ended up buying some beef on the way home. Fel's expression brightened noticeably.

But Shea shook her head at him, committing the scene of the chaotic market to memory. She could tell that the end was near.

That evening, after Fel ate all the beef as expected, Shea went first after leaving the dishes to him. Once she showered and returned to her room, she flopped onto the couch when there was an unexpected call.

She opened the communication line unenthusiastically.

"Hey, Shea Grande. Are you still alive?"

"Hi, Dean Byron. Sadly, I haven't bitten the dust yet."

The sight of her in a bathrobe, wine glass in hand, was undeniably alluring, yet the person on the other end seemed completely unaffected. This was only natural, given that they were family.

"I know, right?" he replied. "Why can't we just die, you and I?"

"Because we're technically not old enough to die yet."

"I'm not sure we'll be able to die even if we reach that age."

Shea's eyes glinted at the meaning behind his seemingly meaningless banter. "Stop it. I'm already feeling down. You're making me want to kill people."

"Understandable."

"So why did you call?" She suddenly remembered something. "Oh right, I need rice."

Dean tilted his head to one side. "Rice? That's random."

"I'm going to make soybean paste stew. I need rice to go with it."

It took Dean a moment to understand what she was saying. It was a very Korean thing to say. "Soybean paste stew? There's no soybean paste in this wor—oh. You made some, didn't you?"

"I almost died making it. I'm never making any again. I made so much that it was twice as hard."

She had remembered reading how to make blocks of fermented soybeans in a comic book long, long ago, so last year, she'd tried to make some. It had been so hard that she'd thought it might kill her. Though the method seemed simple, it took an insane amount of work.

Cooking the beans and mashing them was the easy part. She wasn't meticulous enough to sort through the beans or stir them properly, so she ordered Fel and Lucy to do it. Fel was strong, and mashing the beans was best left to him.

Maybe it was because he was a sword master, but he'd mashed the beans very evenly.

They kept asking her what in the world they were making, but she told them they would see once it was done. They tried to hide their pouting. Shea ignored them.

Then came the hard part. The mashed beans had to be squashed and formed by stepping on them, and that's when things started to get bothersome. There were too many beans. She'd forgotten how much she tended to make when she cooked, and she was forced to step in and do it herself at that point. The lumps of mashed beans had to be cut and tied up with straw rope, which took a long time, but Elias and the others enjoyed it. Behind the café next to the greenhouse, there was a shed for drying things like jerky. Hanging up the blocks of beans and letting them dry was easy.

The real problem was the next part. It was an ordeal. First, the fermented soybean blocks needed to be separated from the soy sauce they'd been sitting in. Then the mold had to be removed and the blocks broken up into small pieces. But Shea couldn't order someone to do that because they didn't know how.

In the end, she had to do it by herself. Her abilities didn't work on mold. It would've been weird if they had, since the result wouldn't have been soybean paste. She went through hell. The broken-up blocks then needed to be soaked in soy sauce and put back in the pot to ferment longer.

Why do I always have to make so much? She'd cursed herself countless times throughout the process.

Maybe the cursing helped, because the resulting soybean paste turned out quite good for someone making it for the first time. She ended up with enough to last a lifetime and a newfound respect for the old ladies on TV who made their own soybean paste and fermented sauces at home. *How did they do this every year?*

"Y-you actually managed to make soybean paste?"

"I'm never making it again. Anyway, that's why I need rice. The rice from your land is the best." She sounded unenthusiastic even as she praised his rice.

But Dean had stopped listening. He raised his hand in the air like an excited child. "I want some, too. I want soybean paste stew, too, please!"

Naturally, his desperation did nothing to move Shea. "Who cares?"

"Hey!"

"Oh, shut up. If you want some, make it yourself."

"You know exactly why I grow food and don't cook, you witch."

"Oh, right." Only then did she remember that Dean Byron was a terrible cook. He had the right recipes, and he followed them to a tee. But for some reason, the resulting dishes were always horrible.

She'd even watched him once. He hadn't done anything wrong. But somehow, his food was always garbage. Their other siblings claimed he was cursed.

But Roux didn't abandon him entirely, because to make up for the curse of being such a terrible cook, Dean was blessed with a green thumb. That's why he started farming. Though the staple grain in the empire was wheat, he grew rice because he suffered the most from homesickness. He also grew wheat of top quality. He had a gift for raising crops. Shea bought wheat elsewhere at times, but most of the flour she used was from Dean.

"I forgot. Sorry."

"Then give me some! *Bwaaah*, I want soybean paste stew too."

Wow, he's actually crying. Shea was impressed. She remembered how desperate he'd been for kimchi, saying that he was sick of western food. When she refused, he'd clung to her until she gave in—that's how Korean his tastebuds still were.

"You can make yourself some beef radish soup, right?"

"No, I can't."

"That's not something to brag about." *It's the easiest thing to make. Just boil beef with radish and some salt in water, then some green onion and crushed garlic. You even grow those. Easy. Why else would you grow rice? What do you even eat it with?*

She couldn't understand him. "Fine, then. I'll make it for you if you come over."

"I'm on my way!"

"Hey, what about the rice? I need rice."

"I'll bring it with me."

Her enthusiasm waned the more eager he sounded. "Fine. So how are your crops doing?"

She was asking whether the ward breaking in the West had affected his harvest. Dean smirked cynically as he replied, "The empire's falling to ruin isn't going to affect us. Of course, my crops are fine. How am I supposed to fulfill my damn role if I can't even have that much?"

"You're right. Makes sense."

It was a very clear answer.

CHAPTER FIFTY-TWO

Meanwhile, the temple wasn't entirely unaffected by recent events.

"The western ward has been destroyed! We may be making the most of this opportunity now, but if the rest of the wards are destroyed, we'll be ruined as well."

Even they knew that this wasn't merely an opportunity to exploit. They doubled down on evangelizing to the masses.

But they were anxious, as well.

"Your Holiness, if all four wards are destroyed, the whole empire will fall. There's no guarantee we'll be safe."

"Wouldn't it be better to join hands with the imperial palace this time?"

Some of the priests advocated for putting their own safety above their greed. Plenty of others disagreed.

"It's the imperial palace's responsibility to worry about the empire. It has nothing to do with us, who serve Roux. We're not tied to the empire. The fall of the empire doesn't automatically mean that the temple will fall along with it."

"Exactly. This is the perfect opportunity to put pressure on the imperial palace, Your Holiness."

Verdel couldn't help but chuckle to himself as he watched this obvious, unsightly display of greed around the pope. *If only they would all die.*

"According to reports from the West, the people there are very unsettled. This is the perfect opportunity to gain more followers."

"We, however, must be mindful of the risks. And manipulating the anxious masses is no easy task."

"But we have a guiding star among us, the one the people have so desperately hoped for."

The way the last priest glanced at Verdel with such confidence was laughable.

Verdel let out a huff of laughter. Everyone nodded in agreement yet failed to notice his reaction. They brimmed with confidence. Verdel had long since given up on them, clucking his tongue at their incomprehensible and unfounded confidence. To him, they seemed even crazier than he was.

"So, what does a great Child of God chosen by Roux think about this catastrophe that has befallen the empire?" asked the pope. He cunningly left out the temple, as if it had nothing to do with the empire.

Verdel wouldn't denounce the pope for it. His cunning was how he'd gained this honored seat to begin with. He decided to proceed with his plans and the reason he was here. "It is fated to happen. Do you think you can stop it, even though you haven't found any of my siblings in years, even though you still don't know whether it was a human, someone from a different species, a natural disaster, or whatever else that caused all this?"

"..."

"The fall of the empire isn't a simple matter, but even if it does fall, it wouldn't affect us," Verdel continued. "Therefore, should we not take this opportunity to aim for more power and authority?"

"What do you mean?"

Verdel held back the impulse to cluck his tongue in annoyance at the pope's stupid, uncomprehending voice. "Currently, the only surviving member of the imperial family is the emperor. But who knows? There may be more survivors, and if that's the case—"

"We must protect them. From the emperor." A wide smile spread across the pope's face as he finally understood what Verdel was saying.

Verdel gave a satisfied smile. Everything was going according to plan. "Yes, and we must raise the stakes and weaken the throne. We have a great debate topic, after all."

"Raise the stakes?"

"The empire in crisis. A suitable topic to gather everyone, don't you think?"

The pope tilted his head until it finally clicked, and his eyes widened. "Is it really possible?"

Verdel confirmed his suspicions with great enthusiasm. "Ah, how many centuries has it been since the last Glorious?"

"...!"

The leaders of the temple widened their eyes in shock.

Verdel gave them the biggest smile they'd ever seen. What he'd been hoping for was finally coming to pass. "May Roux' will be done."

May my will be done.

"Eid, you're doing it again. I told you not to do that!"

Eid was dreaming yet again.

No, he was regaining his memories. He'd finally realized that these dreams were bits of his memories. It seemed so obvious once he stopped denying it. He felt stupid for not realizing it sooner.

He was still getting work done, even though it was difficult now that he was regaining his memory even when awake.

Because you always cried and got angry whenever I prioritized you over everything else, including work.

He worked almost reflexively. Under the circumstances, he couldn't ignore it. He worked like a madman. This didn't mean that he was working like crazy, but...

"Are you all right, sire?"

"When was I ever all right?"

...that he was working while crying and laughing like a madman, as he continued to remember things.

Anyone would've thought he was insane. He himself thought so, too. But he didn't really mind.

"You're unbelievable! Get up! Get uuup!"

I want to keep watching you.

"Maybe you should take a break?"

"I think you need a break more than I do, Ace."

Ace shrugged as he touched his face, haggard from the many nights of overtime they had both pulled. "I'm used to it. I'm fine."

Eid let out an exasperated huff of laughter at Ace's nonchalant criticism. Eid wondered whether he'd become soft, judging by how sassy Ace was being. Not that he hasn't always been that way.

"I must be going easy on you."

"What did you say?" *What? Excuse me?*

Eid could tell he had indeed been going easy on Ace by his reaction. He wasn't quite sure how to describe this feeling. He frowned. Ace's reaction was both natural and yet not at all natural.

"I used to be even more relaxed, once upon a time."

"..."

You probably remember it, as well... since you've been with me nearly every day ever since you were born.

Ace gave him a searching look.

Eid faced him head on.

Ace gave him a peaceful smile, as though he'd risen above it all. "Yes, you did. Although I'll never be able to see you like that again." *Unfortunately.*

Eid knew for certain when he saw the look on Ace's face, which was solemn even though his tone was casual. Ace was aware of everything. He was sure Ace was feigning ignorance and had no intention of telling him the truth, for his and someone else's sake.

Ace Maxwell was like that. He was as clever as he was quick-witted and self-aware, and yet he didn't care about himself very much.

Like a fool.

"Would you like to see me like that again?" Eid already knew the answer. Because the way Ace smiled at him as if in a dream, as if he were about to cry, was...

"So much so that I'd be willing to die for it."

...so much like Eid himself. He couldn't get angry with him.

"You're dismissed," he said dryly.

"Yes, Your Imperial Majesty."

Eid leaned back in his chair and closed his eyes. He could remember quite a few things now, though they were trivial. He knew that she'd worked part-time at the palace, and though she was assigned to the kitchens first, she'd quickly been roped into working in the emperor's quarters.

And the day after she was reassigned was the day they'd met.

As if it was destiny.

She told him later that she really thought she might die, based on the horrifying things she'd heard about him. And he found himself regretting his actions. He wished he hadn't acted like such a madman. Everything he'd done was out of necessity, but no man wants to look bad in front of his lover.

She'd smiled in such a lovely way at the sight of him contemplating this.

One week. One week was enough to fall in love.

To fall in love with her.

He'd fallen for her first. He'd done all kinds of ridiculous things to woo her, all kinds of embarrassing things that he sorely regretted later. He tried to get her attention by acting like a petulant child, telling her she was nothing even as he followed her around every day.

It had been so bad that the kindhearted girl had told him to stop stalking her. His excuse was that she happened to be wherever he was, not that he was following her. Such a pathetic lie.

When he remembered the way he professed his affections for her, not lying for once, he wanted to go back in time and kill himself. It wasn't much of a profession of love, really.

"Come on, why do you keep following me around? What is it? Do you think I'm some kind of spy or something? I'm not that smart, you know. Do I look that smart to you? Shea always tells me I'm a blockhead."

It was a strange thing for her to say, referring to herself. He knew now exactly who she'd been talking about, but back then he was uncharacteristically dumbfounded by the way she fumed at him. He'd never seen her act that way in the month he'd known her.

"A-are you—"

"What? Are you going to kill me? Go ahead, I don't care. Or I'll quit and run away. I'm here for the money, but I'm not that desperate, you know."

"What... What are you..."

He hadn't been able to form a whole sentence at the sight of her. She'd apparently forgotten who he was, judging by how aggressive she was being. As he hesitated, she took the opportunity to go all in and shout more.

"What is it? What do you want from me?"

CHAPTER
FIFTY-THREE

The impact of her outburst was that much greater because her usual demeanor was so mild.

He blurted out an answer without thinking. "Because I like you!"

"Do you really think that's an excuse to—wait, what?"

Even he was surprised. In fact, he was even more surprised than she was. Even as he'd bothered and annoyed her every day, he hadn't realized his own feelings until that moment. But once he expressed them, he was sure. He liked the woman in front of him very, very much.

"I love you, Sistina."

"Wh-what are you saying?"

He laughed out loud at how she flushed bright red. It was truly adorable.

"I'm serious."

"Y-you're teasing me! This is another way of bullying me, right?"

He grinned from ear to ear as he wrapped his arms around the panicking woman. He couldn't help but smile. The happiness blooming inside him made it impossible not to. "You know I'm being serious."

"...!"

As clueless as she was about most things, she'd always been good at telling others' true feelings. There was no way she didn't realize it. She widened her eyes, a deer caught in headlights.

He took his chance. "Do you hate me?"

She let out a long sigh in response. "You can't say that. That's cheating."

And that was enough. He had more than enough of an advantage. He was confident in being able to make her like him as much as he liked her, because she'd changed him so much.

The kiss they had shared then was sweeter and more glorious than anything else in the world. In that moment, he was happy. Sincerely.

He wondered if he had ever been happier in his life.

If there was some way to do it, he wanted to go back in time. Just as Ace had said, *"So much so that I'd be willing to die for it."* But a wish was a wish.

There was something else Eid had realized in the process of regaining his memory. He'd realized why he subconsciously clung to the magic seal that kept him from remembering this part of his past.

"I can't get up."

"Good."

"Eid!"

"You don't need to work. There are more than enough people to take over your job."

Even if it was only in his dreams.

"But it's my job!"

"You're doing something much more important than that."

"I am? What am I doing?"

Even if it was just a little longer.

"Attending the emperor?"

"Ugh."

He wanted to see her. He wanted to meet her, even if only in his dreams.

"Why did you leave me behind?"

Because he knew he couldn't see her any longer.

As he continued to regain his memories and realized how pathetic he was, he began to resent her. "You should have taken me with you."

You knew that a world without you meant nothing to me.

"Where did my lover gooo? He's not showing his face at aaaall. Why does he have to be like thiiis?"

Fel had given up already and continued to work as he ignored Shea's strange singing, but the customers watched her warily.

After things had gone wrong in the West, Edward had gone missing—only to Shea.

The Griffiths, who represented the South, couldn't turn a blind eye to the famine in the West. Edward had taken care of the urgent business at the Ministry of Defense in order to go south to his family's estate and investigate the situation.

Leaving Shea behind. That was the part she was mad about.

Who said I wouldn't go with you? Did you think I'd curse at you for asking? How could you not even ask? She wondered what in the world he thought of her. It was infuriating.

She understood his stupid point of view. He obviously didn't want to get rejected and had probably been worried about inconveniencing her if she went with him. At least that was clear. But just because she understood his thought process didn't mean that it didn't tick her off.

Damn Edward van Griffith. "Just you wait." *I'll give you hell when you get back.*

Everyone in the café flinched at the frightening aura emanating from her. Crossing her today would not end well. Even as they trembled in fear, they ate every last bite of her food and put away their trays before leaving the café.

Shea sighed as she got started on the dishes. "Ugh, that damn bastard."

She gripped a plate tight enough to break it as she violently scrubbed at it, before slamming it down in anger. Her mood was not getting any better. *Why is he wasting so much time? I don't even know how much time we have left—*

"Oh." *Is that why I'm so angry?*

She let out an exasperated laugh as she realized why she was so frustrated and impatient. In the end, she was like him. Like him, she was afraid of losing him. Afraid of losing him yet again. She'd given up so much for it.

"It makes me want to murder someone, father." *Is this what you wanted?*

Sometimes, Shea wondered. Usually, she didn't care to understand. She didn't see the good in it. She scoffed at the idea of racking her brain over something she couldn't understand. But when she was overwhelmed by emotion, she found herself driven by the urge to know, especially after becoming a mother herself.

Most religions depicted a benevolent god, But the truth was far from it. Gods were paradoxical beings that seemed to care for humans but saw them as nothing more than lowly insects. They claimed to love humans but didn't hesitate to plunge them into despair. This was no different for the children of the gods, who were supposedly loved and treasured by their respective gods.

She remembered resenting Roux for it countless times, asking so many times why his love manifested itself in this way.

"And they say parents have a soft spot for their children..."

It was nonsense. *You always took away my happiness, as if you wanted me to fall into despair. As if you wanted me to have no one but you.*

In this life, Shea had cried exactly two times. The first time was when she lost him. The second time was when she lost her parents. There was a saying that real men cried only three times in their lives: when they were born, when they lost their parents, and when they lost their country. It had been exactly like that for her.

You probably won't allow me to cry like that again—because that's what you're like.

And that made her nervous. What if he took him away from her again? He had done it before. But what she feared more than that was...

"I won't even be able to cry over you, you idiot."

So, I can't tell you anything. Because everything might come true if I do.

"Mmph!" Suddenly, she found it hard to breathe. The world went dark. She couldn't see anything.

Just like before.

Are my powers going to leave me again? Anxiety and a sense of loss weighed her down heavily.

Just as she thought she might die from the pressure, a bright light blinded her, and with a loud slam of the door, they brought Shea back to reality.

"Shea, we're here!"

"I want your soybean paste stew."

"Shut up, you're so loud."

"Soybean paaaste!"

"I'm going to stick your head in the paste if you don't stop."

"The rice is so heavy."

"Ugh, why did you come together?" she asked.

Just as they always did.

She couldn't help the smile that crept onto her face at their noisy entrance. "Shut up! You're going to bring the house down."

"Shea!"

"Shea, I'm starving!"

It was a familiar greeting.

Knowing that things would become troublesome if anyone saw them, Shea closed the café before heading into the kitchen to put a pot on the stove. With practiced ease, she mixed bean paste with water, then chopped and added onions, potatoes, and beef. She also generously added the precious tofu.

"Dean Byron, you know how to wash rice, right?"

"Of course!"

"Can he do it without messing up, though?"

"He should be able to do at least *that* much."

In the short moments that Shea left Dean with the rice to go to the greenhouse, everyone went pale as they saw what he was doing to the rice.

They all ran at him.

"Someone stop that bastard!"

"Put it away! How can you mess up even something as simple as washing rice?"

"Let's get rid of it before Shea sees it. If we're not careful, we won't be able to eat anything."

Dean cried out in frustration, having somehow made the rice brown, even though he'd washed it properly.

"Well then, you guys should have jumped in and done it yourselves."

"We didn't think he would be this bad!"

Dean's eyes filled with tears at their exasperation. Who could have imagined that anyone could mess up such a simple task?

Ignoring his grief, they went about getting rid of the ruined rice as quickly as possible. Perhaps he really was cursed. How could someone make white rice into brown rice by washing it? They shook their heads and divided into two teams, one to handle the rice and one to handle Dean.

The person chosen to wash the rice properly was Letis, the Child of Purification. She quickly purified the rice using her God-given abilities. "Whew, the evidence is gone."

"Hey, get up. Get up and look excited for the meal!"

"Got it!"

They all cooperated.

Shea returned to the kitchen. "What did you do?"

"Nothing. Oh, I washed the rice."

"Wow, not bad. I didn't expect you to succccd."

Well, he didn't. Sometimes it was better not to tell the whole truth.

Shea went about cooking the rice and making side dishes.

"Wow, is that tofu? When did you make that?"

"She always complains, but she never skimps out."

"Is she making braised tofu? Or a stir fry?"

"I want it stir-fried!"

"What? Braised tofu is obviously better."

"Just be grateful and eat whatever's put in front of you."

It ended up being stir fry.

Three of the five guests cheered, while the other two despaired. They didn't hide their emotions.

"Hooray!"

"Yes!"

By then, the rice was done, and everyone started to look excited.

"Take these to the table," Shea said.

"Yes, mom," they exclaimed in unison as they went to set the table.

Shea found herself at a loss for words. She'd missed the right time to object to their calling her "mom." She stood stock still as the food was taken from her hands. *I should've told them all to get out.*

Shea let out a small sigh at the sight of them throwing a party with the food they'd taken to the table.

CHAPTER
FIFTY-FOUR

"Hey, move over. I want some, too."

"You haven't eaten yet?"

"It's dinnertime. I thought you came here in time for dinner."

"Oh, right."

Shea glared at them for not thinking of her share. "Do you want a funeral with all this food?"

"We're sorry." They instantly apologized, knowing full well that her quiet threat was completely serious. They couldn't possibly allow all this food to be taken from them now.

Sigh.

She raised her spoon at their quick apology, and everyone grinned widely as they took up their own spoons and went to town.

The feast had begun.

"Hey, don't take two at a time."

"Stop talking while you're chewing. It's gross."

"Shut up! There's no time."

The side dishes went flying, but none of them landed on the ground. Everyone's chopsticks were at the ready, catching everything in midair.

"Just shut up and eat! Like Dean."

"You should tell him to slow down. He's not even chewing."

"Ugh, Dean, you're going to choke to death."

"No regrets!"

"We're the ones who would have to deal with your dead body."

Dean continued to shovel food into his mouth as the others bickered over removing him from the table.

It was pure chaos, reminiscent of a bustling market, effectively ruining her appetite—not that she had much of one to begin with.

She put down her spoon and watched. Even though she wasn't eating, she felt pleased. Maybe she didn't like being alone. Being with her family, as loud as they were, was nice. Maybe it was because she had been lost in the darkness only moments before they arrived.

"Were you beggars in your past lives?" she asked. "You're acting like Noise."

"Hey, we're not that bad. If he were here, we wouldn't even be able to eat."

"It's so weird. He eats elegantly, but the speed at which he eats is unbelievable."

"No one can beat him."

Shea nodded. "That's true." It wasn't hard to agree, based on how recently he'd emptied her entire fridge. She'd had to order in bulk after that. Fortunately, it happened before prices skyrocketed. She was genuinely thankful for that.

He ate way too much.

In what felt like less than ten minutes, all the food was gone. *Did someone hire them to come and steal my food?* Whoever her siblings were living with must have earned a lot of money. Although even that might not be enough.

"Whew, what a great meal."

"I love how Shea always makes so much."

"We can always eat as much as we want."

Shea considered that she might need to work on her tendency to make too much food, though it had never bothered her before.

"I'm so glad we happened to be staying with Dean Byron."

"So that's why you all came together," Shea said. "I thought it was strange."

"Of course. Do you think Dean Byron would actually invite us? He'd rather take the extra food for himself."

Shea nodded, finally understanding why they were here together. *Yup. That's why I thought it was strange that you came together.*

The others leaned back in their chairs, pleased and drowsy.

"I think that's the first time I've had bean paste stew since I was reborn. Why don't they have soybean paste in this world?"

"Because it's a different world, obviously. It's not that bad. We've gotten used to the food here, right?"

"I still miss it sometimes. It's only natural for people to want something different if they always eat the same kind of thing."

"And this guy is seriously homesick."

"Yeah, that makes sense. Anyway, that was so good."

The others nodded as they watched Dean lick his lips as if he wanted more. Then they took out the dessert they'd brought with them. While it was no match for the food at Sangria, they agreed that they couldn't ask Shea to make dessert as well.

Petra used her magic to make some tea while Shea opened a box of oatmeal cookies.

"Ooh, oatmeal cookies?"

"I know you like them," Shea said. "They're easy to make."

"Seriously, it's so strange that you're so talented at baking when you're so lazy."

"Right? It's not like Shea to want to do things that require following exact instructions and measurements. She's usually very lazy. But somehow, she's amazing at baking."

"She seems experienced, too."

"Right? How did you get into baking, Shea?"

Their eyes sparkled with curiosity, even though they tried to conceal it. Shea never talked about her past life.

Those Children of God who were chosen directly by a god were either reborn or lived forever. Those who lived forever were rare, so most of the chosen ones had been reborn. They came from different times and different worlds. In their past lives, the five gathered here had been from Korea or countries with a similar culture.

In other words, they always knew what she was talking about, and their bond was strong. They valued each other for their shared experiences and tended to discuss things they couldn't share with anyone else. They'd all gone through times when they missed their past lives and couldn't get over their memories.

But Shea rarely talked about herself, though it wasn't intentional. They knew she wasn't keeping quiet on purpose, whether it was because she didn't want to remember or she didn't want to be overcome with emotion, which made them all the more curious.

Looking uninterested as she took a bite of an oatmeal cookie, Shea gave them an answer. "It's actually quite simple. I tried hard."

"You tried hard? Why?"

"He really loved sweets. He didn't look like it, but he did."

As she smiled, Shea unbelievably looked like a young woman in love. Even the way she stared wistfully into the distance showed her feelings. They concluded then and there that whoever she was referring to couldn't be a family member or friend.

"It must've been a boyfriend. Wow, so she did date."

"He must've been a brave one if he made her act like that."

After passing judgment on a boyfriend they'd never met, the others wiggled their eyebrows and exchanged a few cheeky comments.

"So, you baked for him a lot, huh?"

"He must've been a nice guy if he changed you that much."

Shea let out a scoff at that. "He was a complete idiot."

It would be hard to find a more idiotic man, she added. She was even grinding her teeth, but even then she looked happy. As if she was showing them how much she loved this man.

"Sounds like a great guy."

"Right? I'm jealous."

"I know you dated. Don't pretend you didn't."

"The problem is that it's past tense."

"Oh man, I'm starting to get angry."

"Right? Me, too."

Father had earned everyone's resentment equally this way. It was horrible of him.

"But Shea is loved above us all, isn't she?"

"Oh, the irony."

"Agreed."

The conversation left them in pain. Trying to ignore the bitter emotions rising up, they changed the topic.

"By the way, he was celebrating that the end was finally near."

"Who?"

"Christian."

Shea's attitude changed at the sound of the name everyone knew.

"Christian? Christian Ruperto? That suicidal maniac?"

"Yup, that guy. I know we all feel like that sometimes, but he's got some real issues."

"The end is coming? Does that mean we're going to die? Really?"

Death for them was different from the kind of death a suicidal maniac might envision. And the sentiment didn't sound very believable coming from a suicidal maniac.

"For real this time?"

Jess, who had been quietly eating a cookie, spoke up. "I saw him the other day, and it seems to be true. I even applauded him for finally getting what he wished for."

Shea thought neither the suicidal maniac cheering for the end nor the person applauding him for it were in their right minds. She didn't bother pointing it out. It wasn't her business. Besides, she would have applauded him too. It was all you could do for someone who wanted to die but couldn't.

"When are we going to get our turn?" Rose sounded wistful.

Everyone, including Shea, gave her a sympathetic smirk. None of them wanted to die, but they were a little jealous. Death for them was something that was granted, not something that came naturally. It was like a gift when finally achieved.

"It's time to sing the requiem soon."

"You should practice your singing."

"We're not the ones singing it."

"We could sing along."

"Oh, shut up."

Listening to their squabbling, Shea began to reminisce, maybe because she was in the company of those who knew she'd been reborn.

It had been well past twenty years since she her last life. She'd been killed at eighteen or nineteen in her past life, so she'd lived as Shea much longer now. The family in her past life had been so terrible that she considered them toxic waste, so her true family was Shea Grande's family. They'd shown her the true meaning of family.

Despite their eccentricities and quirks, they loved her very much.

CHAPTER FIFTY-FIVE

In any case, Shea's past life didn't mean much to her.

In the novels she used to read, those who were reborn would often become lost, unable to differentiate between their past lives and their new lives in another world, or they might ruin their lives by staying caught up in the past. Because her own past life didn't mean much to her, she'd been able to adjust to reality faster than her siblings. The past was the past, and today was today.

The only thing that disturbed that clear delineation was *him*, probably because he'd been the most meaningful part of her past life. She'd given up on it already, and yet it made her scoff every time she thought about it.

Because she was so stupid. Every time, no matter how many times it happened, they could never have their happily ever after. It was almost disgusting; even a curse wouldn't be this bad. And yet, she'd stupidly decided to be foolish again, valuing each day with him and going through the cycle once again. She had worked so hard to earn this time with him, and yet here she was, wasting it.

Stupid Edward van Griffith. "Freaking bastard."

"What was that?"

"A sudden bout of anger at my clueless boyfriend."

They reacted immediately at her casual reply.

"Wait, so it's true that you're dating?"

"I thought that bastard Noise was lying."

She lifted her head. "Oh, so that bastard went around telling everybody about it?"

"You shouldn't have let him know, if you were trying to keep it a secret."

"He's always so lazy, but when it comes to things like this, he's quicker than a bullet."

You know that. Shea placed her hand on her forehead at the relentless responses. *That blabbermouth bastard.* She hadn't exactly been trying to hide it, but she wasn't keen on the news traveling so fast.

Fresh anger bubbled up but quickly dissipated again. "Right. What did I expect from that bastard?"

The others smiled warmly at her. "So, you really like this boyfriend of yours, huh?"

She sighed at the question, laden with all their past experiences and emotions, and opened her heart to them. "Why else would I do all this? You know me."

"True. So, what do you like about him?"

What do I like about him? It was a question she'd gotten a lot, even in her past life. Maybe it was a standard question you were asked when you started dating someone. Every time she was asked this question, she was never able to come up with a proper answer.

No matter what he looks like, he's always...

"The fact that he's so consistently dumb."

...the same. To me. And that idiot would never know how satisfying that one, simple thing is to me.

And the fact that she felt so empty without him here.

She wondered what he was doing out there without her. "I'm annoyed."

"Oh, so you're annoyed because you haven't seen your boyfriend in a while."

"Under the current circumstances, I suppose he can't spend one hundred percent of his time on his lover, regardless of his status."

Shea furrowed her eyebrows at this undeniable fact. "Ugh, why did things have to get so annoying?"

"That includes our damn colleague, doesn't it?"

Shea let out another snort. "That's why it's even more annoying. All he did was scoff when I gave him advice."

They nodded. Everyone agreed that his fate was the result of his own actions, as cruel as that might sound. "He only realized how important your advice was after he lost everything.”

“That’s why he went insane.”

What a pity. As much as she was devoid of emotional depth, she could still be sympathetic. A sympathetic smile was as far as her sympathy went.

“No one’s going to stop him, though.”

“Of course not.”

Humans were the ones who started everything to begin with. *So why should we have to solve their problems for them? They ought to take responsibility for their own actions.* “I have no intention of meddling in the affairs of humans. They got themselves into this mess.”

“They can clean up their own shit.”

Everyone burst out laughing at the rude but true comment.

Shea laughed too. “My boyfriend looks like an idiot for running around like a fool.”

“Is he a noble? Then he has no choice.”

“Oh, so that’s why you were so annoyed.”

“You’re not going to interfere, though, are you?”

Shea replied with an ominous smirk. “Of course not.”

They suddenly felt bad for her boyfriend. *Tsk, tsk. It's his own fault for falling for someone like Shea. Maybe it was fated, but still.*

It was his own fault for falling for her. He must've gone through an entire series of hoops to get past Shea's walls. She wasn't the type of woman to fall for someone easily. And if he'd broken through those walls to date her, it probably meant he loved every part of her.

Taking that thought as comfort, they said no more.

Shea, who had been cursing to herself again as if her anger were coming back, raised her head.

"What is it?"

They were caught off guard. Shea wore an expression they'd never seen before.

Unaware of their confusion, she spoke up. "It's the idiot."

"Huh?" *Who's the idiot?*

They tilted their heads in confusion at her puzzling words.

Shea's face brightened like a warm spring day. "The idiot's coming!"

Who in the world?

They looked at Shea with stunned faces, but she ignored them, leaped to her feet, and ran to the door. She threw open the door and stepped outside to find Edward, who looked surprised by her sudden appearance. He'd been hesitating to knock because it was late at night.

"Shea?"

She ran into his arms and squeezed him tightly.

"Shea?" He looked flustered by the unexpected greeting.

She refused to let him go. "What took you so long?"

The sobs barely concealed in her voice were more sincere than anything she could have said.

He smiled brightly as he hugged her back. "I'm back."

They were, undoubtedly, two lovebirds deeply in love.

The others, witnessing this scene against their will, pulled faces.

"Umm, this is nice and all, but why am I so ticked off?"

"It's not like I don't have my own lov—oh, I guess I don't. Damn it."

"I want to date, too. This is annoying to watch. Hmph."

Though they grumbled, they looked quite happy. They, too, loved Shea.

"She looks happy. I'm glad."

On the outskirts of the capital, in the middle of the secret forest, lay the meeting place for the Glorious Assembly. It had been a few hundred years since anyone had entered this place, which stood empty when there wasn't an assembly.

Lilith, the fairy and mascot of Glorious who acted in Roux' name and only appeared before guests who had the right to be there, appeared before the guest to welcome him. "Welcome, Verdel Isis Hydia of Indulgence, the ninth Child of God. May Roux' blessing always be with you."

"You haven't changed at all, Lily."

"Though many things may change, it is part of my nature to stay unchanging."

Verdel's lips curled into a bitter smile at her machinelike reply. For a brief moment, he envied the little fairy before him. Maybe if he had been this perfect, he wouldn't have broken. *Father should have chosen someone like her as his child, not me. If he wasn't going to allow any room for mistakes.*

He gathered himself, putting aside his bitterness. It was too late to turn back, and he had no intention of doing so. All he could do was move forward without hesitation. "As one of the children of Roux, I would like to exert my authority to hold a Glorious Assembly."

Lilith considered him a moment. "May I see your assembly proposal?"

"Here." He handed the paper he'd prepared beforehand. She made it float in the air.

Whoosh!

The letters on the paper glowed golden and began to appear in the air, lighting up and then disappearing.

"Your proposal has been accepted," she said. "The Glorious Assembly will be held in one week. I shall send out an invitation to the representatives of the empire and to each Child of God."

"Thank you."

Lilith eyed Verdel quietly. "Once the invitations are sent out, they cannot be taken back. Are you sure you will not regret it?"

It was uncharacteristically courteous of her. Lilith wasn't someone who gave people a chance to reconsider.

Verdel gave her a look of surprise.

She looked at him without emotion, as if she had no other expression to show. "Of course."

It was a lie. His gut told him it was. But Verdel ignored his gut feeling and answered her confidently, putting on the arrogant facade that was like a weapon to him. It was his way of strengthening his own resolve.

He had already regretted his actions countless times—so many times, in fact, that he was nothing but an empty husk. He could no longer regret anything. Even if he could, he had regretted so many things that this would be merely another regret on the mountain of past regrets. It would make no difference.

It was why he was able to do something so insane.

Verdel gave her a cynical smile.

Lilith found herself unable to say anything more at the sight of his fragile smile. With an unchanging expression, she tore up the paper he'd given her.

This triggered some sort of magic. Golden light shot throughout the meeting place. The beads of light gathered in several spots, manifesting into birdlike shapes that flew off.

They were invitations.

"Your proposal has been accepted. I sincerely hope that this will be a blessing for you."

It was the start of another Glorious Assembly.

The communication device lit up. It was a signal.

"Ugh, what now?" Shea wriggled an arm from under the covers and placed her hand over the communication device.

CHAPTER FIFTY-SIX

As Shea reached for the communication device, her blanket slid from her shoulders, revealing her bare torso. She looked around, unconcerned. Her lover had reluctantly torn himself away a few hours after sunrise. She could still feel the goodbye kiss, even through the haze of sleepiness. As a stand-in for the Minister of Defense, he was naturally busy, but she couldn't help feeling disappointed that he had to leave.

Putting aside her discontent, she picked up her bathrobe, which was splayed across the floor.

The silhouette of a person appeared on the communication device. "Oh. I see my timing is impeccable."

Noel found himself uncharacteristically flustered. He hadn't contacted Shea in a while, and now he was faced with the sight of her bare back. Even after years of working by her side and getting used to her liberal attitude about exposing her skin, her beauty was incredible.

Shea was surprised to see that he was still flustered at the sight of her bare skin and decided to tease him a little. "Why, did you miss me?"

"Not at all. I would like to die of old age."

"Ha. Who's going to kill you for looking at me?"

Noel couldn't bring himself to say the words "your boyfriend," so he didn't. *That's right.* Girlfriends thought they knew their boyfriends well, but sometimes they were the most clueless about them. This was one of those cases.

"First, as per your order, we've completed the task of dividing the food in Grande into that which must be consumed soon and that which can be stored," he began. "This catastrophe hasn't affected our territory significantly, so the process went smoothly. The problem is that other territories have realized we're doing well, and they've been asking for aid."

"Tell them to piss off."

"I already did. And, just as you ordered, we've filled the storage warehouses to the brim. Our territory should be free of food issues for at least three years."

Under different circumstances, this news would have been enough to satisfy her. But Shea caught a crucial detail. "That number is based on our current population, right?"

"Yes. I was just about to tell you," he grumbled inwardly at her refusal to do any work herself—despite having the insight and ability. After all, she had predicted the famine. She was clearly made to rule a territory. *So why do you keep denying it?*

His face didn't betray his complaints. It was all thanks to Shea's teachings.

"There are already over five hundred refugees requesting to move to our territory," he said. "We have currently put all requests on hold with the excuse of our ruler being absent, but—"

"They must be rioting, complaining about why we won't let them in. Grande has been generous toward its newcomers the past three years."

"Yes. I believe a riot is imminent. The citizens are starting to get worried. They're aware of the fact that the food supply is limited, and if many refugees enter, the crime rate will go up, as well."

"That's why I've always put a limit on how many people can move in," she said. "It's obvious what will happen if we accept too many at once. If we can't take care of them, they'll only become a burden."

Noel thought back to how he'd reacted to this cold but realistic policy of hers in the past. He lowered his head in shame. "At first, I was against it because I was concerned about public opinion, but now I'm eternally grateful you didn't listen to my insane advice."

"Whatever. Grande won't take in any more people. We can't support them, right?"

"That's true, but it won't make us look good." Noel's head was already starting to hurt, thinking about the nonsensical complaints they would have to endure about how they were being selfish and casting away helpless and powerless people.

Shea knew how he felt, but she remained stern. "So what? Is looking good going to feed anyone? The outcome of letting them in is obvious. We have to watch out for our own people. There's no need for anyone to kick the bucket. Other territories can do what they want, but I have no intention of taking part in it. I didn't even want to rule a territory—but as long as I do, I have a responsibility to my citizens. My reputation might suffer, but I'm going to put my own people first. Who cares if others point fingers at me? I certainly don't."

Noel didn't have anything else to add. "I understand."

Shea could tell that while he understood her reasoning, he couldn't help a slight sense of guilt. She gave him a bittersweet smile. Noel looked like someone who would be calculating and coldhearted, yet he was such a softie. "Noel."

"Yes, Shea."

"Protect yourself."

"Pardon?"

"Don't let anyone take anything from you—the things you have, the person you are. Don't let anything be taken from you. From now on, countless people are going to beg, threaten, or do whatever it takes to take away what's yours. Humans turn into beasts in a heartbeat when it comes to greed. You know this."

"Shea."

"This world has nothing more to give. Resources are limited, and everyone will throw morals and conscience to the curb to try and obtain them. You must prepare yourself. I will do nothing, and I'll stay exactly the same way as I am now. I'm going to let this change happen. So, Noel, think hard about what you must do to survive."

It was too much of a speech to be considered idle talk and too cruel to be considered genuine advice. Especially because he knew that Shea never gave empty advice, and she never joked about these kinds of things. He knew she was telling him this for his own good.

Shea clucked her tongue at him. "You fool."

You're hopeless.

Meanwhile, Edward, who had struggled to tear himself away from Shea that morning to go to work, was reporting to his superior. He carried a bit of an attitude today—because he detested being away from his lover even for a second.

"I'll summarize matters in one sentence," Edward said.

"Stop it."

"It's a complete mess."

"I said, stop it."

Eid let out a sigh at Edward's grouchy report. Nothing was going the way he wanted it to. He'd never wanted to become emperor, and he was sick of all the things he had to deal with year after year. The emperor was supposed to be on top of the world and command it according to his will. But somehow, his life was far from that.

He gritted his teeth in frustration. The situation was upsetting enough already, and to top it off, all this had to happen when he was emperor, as he was in the process of losing his mind to the curse.

He wanted it to end. He didn't care about the empire anymore. *None of it matters.*

"Edward, I have a question for you," he said.

"Go ahead, Your Imperial Majesty." When he heard how much strength and determination the emperor's voice had lost, Edward put aside his resentment and bowed his head.

"So, now there are two left. If all those damn wards were to be destroyed, do you think this empire can survive?"

"…"

Edward had a hard time answering. He, too, had witnessed the cruelty and wickedness of humanity, had been content with the present, and had watched the pitiful conduct of humans who wanted to settle for the present as well. Judging from the way everyone was panicking, the clear answer to the emperor's question was no. It was clear that people would blame anyone but themselves, beg the gods for help, justify stealing, and eventually hit rock bottom.

Like Eid, Edward didn't have a very high opinion of the masses. And yet, he hesitated, because there was someone he wanted to enjoy life with. A peaceful life.

"It's hard to predict how humans will change," Edward said. "They've survived this far, so I expect them to find ways to continue to do so."

"My, how optimistic." Eid smirked coldly at Edward's uncharacteristic reply. But he was actually laughing at himself. "That's very different from what I think."

"…"

"I just want it to end quickly."

Eid didn't care about life any longer. What he'd lived for had disappeared long ago. Even back when his memory had been locked away, there hadn't been any meaning to his life. The days of having something to live for were long gone.

He wouldn't really mind dying.

But he couldn't simply die. The woman he barely remembered wouldn't have wanted him to. And so, instead, he wished for it to end soon—so he could finally meet her again.

"Eid Roux Vencroft."

"What?"

"Do you wish to die?"

"I'm not sure." Perhaps it was because he wasn't sure he'd meet her again in death. What was he supposed to do if he died but she wasn't there?

Only then did he realize: It was this fear that kept him from dying. Not because she wouldn't have wanted him to.

Because I'll always be selfish and pathetic.

"Get a grip." Edward sharply called him back to reality.

"I suppose I should."

"You still have duties to fulfill." That was why he couldn't die yet, Edward added.

Eid found himself envying his friend. *I wish I could say things with such determination. Like you. I wish I could've said it back then.*

"Right. I suppose I am still the emperor." He wished that were all that was demanded of him. If they wanted more, then—

"Sire!"

"What is it? Has another guardian stone been destroyed?"

"No, sire. An invitation has arrived."

"Are you honestly coming to me with that kind of nonsense right now—"

"It is an invitation announcing that a Glorious Assembly is to be held. We are certain it is the real thing."

I don't care if it's a ghost. It doesn't matter.

CHAPTER
FIFTY-SEVEN

"What?" Eid barked.

Edward gaped. "What did you just—"

"It's the real deal, the first Glorious in three hundred years. The pope is urgently requesting an audience with you, Your Imperial Majesty."

Return to me, even as a ghost.

And just as Eid received his invitation to the first Glorious Assembly in three hundred years, the others also received their own invitations.

"Damn it, what now?"

"Oh, my—that's so pretty, darling."

"What is it?"

"Darling?"

"Ugh, damn it." One of the recipients grimaced and cursed, as if the sight of an invitation floating in the air annoyed rather than awed him.

"Sir?"

Sigh.

"What in the world—ouch! Hot!"

"I knew that was going to happen. You zoned out."

"Shut up. Aw man, my hair." One of them burned his hair because he'd stood in a daze at the unexpected news.

"There it is, as I expected. I really don't want to be told off, though."

"You need to be told off."

"Excuse me? I am the wind. The wind blows past everyone. How could you scold the wind? That's ridiculous."

"Whatever."

And one of them sought to escape the reality that had finally come true.

Though their reactions were different, they all thought the same thing: None of them welcomed the message. There was a reason they called each other family, even though none of them were related by blood. Though they had their differences, they all thought the same.

"Damn it."

Just like Shea.

"You're cursing first thing in the morning?"

Shea grimaced as soon as she saw the invitation unfold before her. She fought the urge to rip it to pieces because she knew very well that would accomplish nothing. She grabbed it, but her grimace didn't fade. She somehow felt like she'd lost. It was a feeling she was used to, but it still felt terrible.

Fel, who'd been preparing to open the café, told her off for cursing.

"It sucks every time." These invitations never made her happy. She wished they would leave her alone.

The invitation crumpled in on itself as she clenched her fists, as if it reflected her feelings.

Those who knew what the invitation was for would have gasped in horror, but Fel said nothing. He was more concerned about Shea than the invitation. He'd learned far too late, when he'd already lost everything, that power couldn't save everyone and that you could try as hard as you wanted and still not achieve your goals. But learning this had meant nothing, because by that time he hadn't had anything left to let him correct his mistakes and start over.

After that day, Fel felt empty inside to the extent that his title as the top sword master no longer meant anything.

But there was a reason he hadn't ended his meaningless life. He wanted to see how her life would end. The weight on her shoulders was much heavier than his, and while she was much stronger, she'd also lost much more. And yet, she never gave up.

He wanted to see how her end would differ from his. She had lost far more than he had, yet she continued to forge ahead and live life. In contrast, he had lost too much and no longer had enough heart left to draw hope from observing her. It was already too late for him. Now, all he desired was to stay by her side, the person who was so similar yet so distinct from him, and witness how her final moments would unfold.

And as he spent more time with her, Fel found himself hoping, "But you'll still go on, won't you?"

"Of course."

Hoping that she, who was so much more powerful, so much greater than him...

"Nothing changes if I stand still. I've had enough of that."

...wouldn't end up the same as him.

"Fel."

"Yes, mistress."

"Get ready. Things are about to get busy."

Even if that means offering myself up, as empty as I am.

"As you wish."

"As the proposal of a Child of God has been deemed acceptable, we call you to participate in the Glorious Assembly at the center of this world. The Glorious Assembly decides on grave matters concerning this world by bringing together the opinions of the miracle workers chosen by the Great God Roux and under his jurisdiction. Those who have received this invitation and are not Children of God have a duty to observe the debate and implement its decisions. Therefore, you must attend the assembly with a serious mindset."

"..."

Ace's expression was neutral, as if he'd given up or anticipated this. He finished reading the invitation out loud. The most powerful man in the empire, the emperor, had thrown it in his direction, saying that he didn't even want to read it. Eid slumped in his chair as if he no longer cared about anything. He looked up lazily at Edward as soon as Ace finished reading.

Edward glared at the emperor, obviously not very appreciative of his attitude, and placed his head in his hands in frustration. "So, this is—"

"An invitation to the Glorious Assembly. To be held one week from now."

"Whew. A week?"

Simply attending the event wasn't all there was to it. There was a mountain of work ahead of them. There'd be no going home for anyone working in the imperial palace, not next week or in the foreseeable future.

Not that they'd been going home often lately, and that included the man who'd started dating someone. The long sigh that came from deep within his soul accurately expressed what everyone was feeling.

"What will you do, sire?" Ace set the invitation in front of the emperor.

"What else can I do? I'll attend."

"You know there's more to it."

"Still, it's not as if we have a choice." Eid fiddled with the corner of the invitation. "I feel like maybe Roux is so sick of our pleading, whining, and shouting that he dumped us on one of his children."

"Sire—"

"What? Let's be honest. We're all thinking it, aren't we?"

"…"

"That's what I'm thinking, at least."

He was sick of it. His words sounded heavy, and the others couldn't fathom how much emotion was behind them. "You would think they'd be satisfied by now, but humans don't know when to stop. It's not like they'll die instantly without this blessing. They're simply losing what wasn't theirs to begin with."

"They say it's worse to bless someone, only to take it back later."

"That's true, no matter how old you are. It's the same. It applies to everyone. Especially to oneself."

Edward shook his head, putting an end to a conversation that was obviously coming from a twisted, disturbed mind. "I'm going to go back to work, sire, so that your reign may be peaceful and prosperous."

"There's no hope for that now," Eid said, "so don't overwork yourself."

"And yet, you're working harder than anybody."

Eid tilted his head, as if he couldn't understand why he was working so hard, either. The more he thought about it, the more it seemed like a mystery. "You're right. I don't even know why I bother. It's not like I'm very attached to this empire or anything."

So why did I work so hard?

In the end, Edward and Ace had nothing more to say. They exited the office in shared silence.

Edward couldn't wrap his head around why Ace was acting this way. The Ace he knew wouldn't back off. The fact that this man, who constantly told off the emperor and scolded him for every little thing, was keeping quiet meant that there was a reason for it.

Though they'd been friends since they were born, Edward had spent most of his childhood at the Griffith estate, unlike Ace, who'd stayed at Eid's side. He'd left for short periods every now and then, but it was only when his parents left on another lengthy honeymoon and left him as a substitute Minister of Defense that he moved to the capital. Edward had been gone too long to know everything.

It was times like this that he regretted not coming back sooner. Perhaps he should've visited more often or moved to the capital sooner. It wasn't as though living at the estate had been that good.

"How long have I lived here?" He thought about this every day, whenever he saw Shea.

"Since I was born, probably. The only reason I ever left was because of school." Ever since he'd found out that Shea had lived in the capital since she was young.

"As you know, I didn't even know about the territory I had received, so I never lived there. And once I found out, it had been settled already, so I didn't have to do much." When he first heard her say this, he'd tried his best to appear unaffected while he despaired on the inside.

Why in the world was I cooped up in that damn estate for so long? It wasn't as though it had anything valuable in it. If he'd moved to the capital sooner, he would've met her sooner.

He regretted it all. Then again, even the air tasted sweeter when it had touched Shea. The world he'd known before he met her couldn't be compared to the one he knew now.

CHAPTER FIFTY-EIGHT

Her presence alone had changed Edward's world. It was only natural that he regretted not meeting her sooner. He was aware of how crazy this sounded, but if that's what it took to keep her by his side...

That's what it took to get your attention in the first place. I have to put my all into getting your attention. Otherwise, you'd never even look at me. You would shake off your regret and turn away.

"Don't go. This isn't what I wanted. Please."

"Ugh." A memory flashed through his head, a memory he didn't remember but was sure had happened. The emotions in his voice were clear and real to him now.

"Don't leave me. I'll do anything." He'd begged her not to leave him. His voice was heartbreaking.

Before he could wonder where this memory came from, his heart achingly responded, leaving no room for thought. Why did he feel like this? It felt so real.

"Edward! Why did you stop all of a sudden? Are you feeling all right?"

He regained his senses at the sound of his name and looked up. Ace was looking at him as if asking why he was acting as crazy as the emperor.

Even as he saw Ace's reaction, Edward was suddenly no longer concerned with what they'd both been thinking about. "I'm fine."

He missed Shea very much.

That evening, Shea sat lost in thought by the crumpled invitation, tapping it with one finger.

When Fel saw her receive the invitation, she cursed and crumpled it up as if it were nothing. But it wasn't *nothing*. She had only pretended not to care so he wouldn't worry.

It was a Glorious Assembly.

That in itself wasn't the issue; it was only a bunch of people gathering together. Admittedly, it had been a long time since she'd seen the others, but that wasn't what made her anxious. The problem was that the end was near, and even though that didn't really matter to her, it bothered her because of her stupid friend.

"Damn you, Sistina Illid."

Her stupid friend, who'd been so hopelessly kindhearted and yet never listened to Shea. The girl Shea couldn't turn a blind eye to because she was so wonderful, even though that meant countless headaches. The damn girl who'd left the world first but who was still causing Shea so much trouble.

Why did you have to leave behind so many problems if you were going to leave so soon?

"Ugh, my head hurts."

Technically, the man Sistina left behind posed the biggest problem, but Shea was more concerned about her son. There were truths in this world better left unknown, and Shea had no intention of burdening Elias with facts he didn't need. Despite her best efforts, the son she raised was as kind and gentle as his biological mother and would be hurt when he discovered the truth.

Shea scoffed at herself for worrying about this. *Look at me, acting like a real mother.* She'd been forced into the role. She'd always thought the term "mother" would never suit her.

And look at the trouble you've gotten me into.

The problem was that her true identity might be found out because of this. That would be incredibly annoying. *I can't believe I'm going through all this trouble just because I tried to treat my friend well.*

You seriously need to thank me on your knees, even in death.

"Ugh, I have more than enough on my plate already because of the price I have to pay."

And yet, things kept piling on. Life was supposed to be full of surprises, and she had done her best to keep going, but she had yet to see any glimmer of hope manifest in her life.

"Shea!"

The only light she'd ever known had returned to her, but her life itself was still in darkness. It was only getting darker. She was tied to a pact with many secrets to keep, and in order to fulfill her end of the deal, she had to keep those secrets safe.

What a pathetic life. Nothing had gone the way she wanted. She didn't even ask for much.

"Shea!"

All she wanted...

"Shea. Shea. Shea."

"Stop calling my name!"

"Shea."

...was to keep hearing that voice.

She didn't think that was unreasonable. It was such a small, insignificant wish. It really wasn't that grand.

"Why am I denied such a small thing?"

Tap.

The precious invitation gently hit the floor.

Anyone else would have gasped in horror—that's how valuable it was. But to Shea, the invitation, worth a thousand gold, was nothing but a piece of paper. She was allowed to treat it as such, which made it all the more ironic.

"This is so easy for him."

And yet, he refused to grant her small wish. The saying that mere humans couldn't understand the minds of gods had never been more relatable.

Anger bubbled up, and the thought of attempting a grand escape bloomed. She knew it was nonsense, but as she continued to think about it, it sounded more and more tempting.

"Should I run away?"

She didn't realize she'd said it out loud until she heard something behind her that raised her hackles.

"Are you going somewhere?"

"Yikes!" she squeaked.

She'd never been so surprised as to let out a sound like that. The timing and sound of his voice had been scarier than something from a horror movie. Heart thumping wildly, she couldn't help but raise her voice in anger. "Hey, make some noise next time! I almost lost my baby."

"...!"

"...?"

"Y-you're pregnant?!"

"..."

She was speechless. *What is wrong with him?!* Only an idiot like him would take such an exaggerated figure of speech literally. It was exasperating. *How could he think I was being serious?* And even if she had, she wondered if anyone would have taken her literally, given the context. The world was vast, and its inhabitants were numerous and diverse, yet she had no desire to discover whether anyone was truly that foolish.

"No, that's not what I meant." *Ever heard of a figure of speech?* She gave up explaining it. She couldn't see why she should have to.

Fortunately, he wasn't a completely lost case, because he finally came to his senses and was now acting embarrassed. If he hadn't, she might've kicked him to the curb.

Not that she hadn't done that before.

The problem was that she couldn't leave him there.

As she reviewed their relationship in her head, Edward flopped onto the floor, aristocratic decorum out the window. "I was so scared."

"Because of the baby thing?"

"No—but that was shocking, too."

His honest answer had her at a loss for words. He'd always been surprisingly honest, but every time something like this happened, she found herself amazed yet again.

Maybe it was because she could never be honest. Then again, it was probably her own fault for being soft toward him. "What were you scared of, then?"

"That you might leave."

"What?"

He covered his face with his hands, like someone scared out of his mind. "That you might disappear." *And leave me behind.*

"...!"

His unexpected answer shocked her. She'd spoken out of anger, but she never imagined he'd take it like this.

But from his point of view, it was only natural. His hands trembled, and he stared at them as if confused as to why they were shaking, his eyes full of terror.

Shea could tell that even if his head didn't remember it, his body did: In the end, she'd always left him, even though it was for his own good. Because he was so foolish and lovely, he preferred to die alongside her instead of agreeing with her decision.

But unlike you, I'm selfish and arrogant, and I didn't want you to make your own decision.

"..."

She'd had no other choice, but even if she could go back, she knew she would've made the same choice. *Because I'm hopeless.*

But when she saw him like this, she did regret it. Just a little. It made her wonder. She wondered what would've changed if she'd chosen differently.

Even though she knew she never would.

"Hey," she began.

"Yes?"

But there was one thing she didn't regret one bit. "Look at me."

"I am."

"Stop lying and look at me." Regardless of her wishes, she was bound by a pact. For her whole cursed life, she would always have to keep these secrets, whether by lying or deception.

"Okay."

"I'm not going anywhere without you." *Even though you're the very reason my life is so cursed. Still...*

"..."

"Where would I go without you, you dummy?"

I don't regret bringing this idiot back to life, father.

Billy shuddered all over with cold, drenched to the bone. They had to dive to reach this underwater cave in the East. "I told you I hate water."

Cedric sounded carefree as he answered. "No worries. I don't like it that much, either."

"That's a lie."

"Aw man, I thought I had you." Cedric laughed and kept walking.

Billy griped about how he could tell such a blatant lie, having been by Cedric's side for so many years and knowing him all too well. While the constant nagging might have annoyed anyone else, Billy kept Cedric grounded in reality. Without an anchor, someone to hold him down, he would have left this world without a second thought.

That wouldn't be so bad—and it was what a certain someone was hoping for—but it wasn't time for that. Just yet.

FIFTY-NINE

"Are you sure it's here?" It was a strange place to keep a guardian stone. If it were to collapse, the ward would be destroyed as well. Billy wondered why it was kept here and whether it truly was in this location.

Cedric was thinking the same thing. "It might be hard to believe, but Verdel himself said so. It has to be here. I heard that the Children of God gain all the knowledge of this world once they're chosen. And even if that's not true, they can probably sense the guardian stones—since they were made by one of their own kind."

"They sound ridiculously powerful."

"You can't compare the Children of God to humans. They might be humans, but they're actually not. Even if they wish to remain human, their father won't allow it. He loves to give them 'special treatment,' you see."

It was hard to say whether that treatment really was "special." Cedric had to agree that it wasn't. He thought it was more of a curse than a blessing. Of the several Children of God he'd met, none of them wanted it. It couldn't be called a blessing when they themselves never made use of it and begged their father to take it back.

"That reminds me," Billy said. "I heard that the Children of God never die. Is that true?"

"It's okay to ask me, but if you ever miraculously happen to come across a Child of God, you should never bring that up."

"Why not?"

"Your head will go flying before you can get an answer. It's taboo to talk about." Cedric hadn't dared to ask Shea but had brought it up with Verdel once. He'd nearly lost his life.

But Billy didn't understand why Cedric was giving him this advice. "Why? Isn't that a good thing? It means you live forever, right?"

It was the goal of everyone in power, the fundamental desire of all humanity. Cedric wondered whether most people thought this way or whether Billy was particularly naive. "Most humans live less than a hundred years."

"True."

"Living longer than that without aging means being excluded and hated by other humans, Billy. People tend to reject anything different, especially if that difference comes from being chosen by a god. That's how it is now, right?"

"Oh."

Though human reactions to the Children of God were diverse—there were those who wanted to use them, those who were in awe of them, and those who worshipped them—no one considered them human.

"They don't like meddling or interfering," Cedric said. "They prefer to blend in and watch things go by. But countless people ask why they won't use their God-given powers for humans, why they won't help humans specifically."

"..."

"That's why they never reveal their identities. They have nothing to gain from being exposed. They're clever and wise, and they never step forward of their own accord. They only make an appearance when they're forced to, despite their wishes."

"For something like the Glorious Assembly?"

Cedric nodded. "Technically, that's the only example. They say they don't care if the world falls to ruin."

"That's inhuman."

"It's because of humans that they've become that way. Humans must deal with the consequences."

There were humans out there who also didn't care about the fate of the world, some even worse. And yet, everyone judged the Children of God for being coldhearted because they had more power, as if they weren't aware that judging them only made them care less.

Before he became who he was today, Cedric had been no different from Billy. When he faced the Children of God, he was forced to realize how pathetic and inconsequential he was. He hadn't been able to say anything then. Humans had no right to even speak to them.

"And they aren't immortal."

"Huh? They're not?"

"They can't end their lives on their own. Even if they ask someone else do it, even if they wish to. They can only die when their fate has decided it's time."

"Oh. Well, that's a bit—"

"It's a curse. So, if you come across any of them, don't bring it up. How much anger do you think they carry because they can't die even if they wish to?"

It wasn't something an average person could even imagine. Death was the great equalizer, fair and merciful to all, taking lives without rhyme or reason—but even that didn't apply to the Children of God. The gods didn't grant them death easily, even if they went on a rampage, determined to end this world. They couldn't possess what came so naturally and inevitably to everyone else.

When all of creation had the right to end their lives, could those who weren't given this right truly be called free?

The Children of God were thus tied down, as much as it seemed that they lived freely.

"I guess I should watch my mouth." Billy nodded thoughtfully, adding that silence was sometimes the best course of action.

Cedric offered a few words of comfort. Billy was taking this a bit too seriously. "Don't worry about it too much. You'll most likely never meet them."

"Oh. Right." Billy shot him a glare as if to say Cedric should've clarified that first.

Cedric ignored him with practiced ease and came to a halt.

"Ooh, is that...?"

"The ruby of the East. A blood-red jewel in the middle of the deep blue sea. A fantastic contrast."

A clear, deep red ruby floated in the middle of the water, its light shining out magnificently. The sight was so beautiful that they found themselves at a loss for words.

"No one seems to be guarding this one," Billy said.

"There aren't many who could even reach this place, anyway."

Billy shuddered at the thought of the ridiculous challenges they had to go through to come here. "Of course, there aren't. You can't treat this place the same as those other places you can simply walk to. I nearly drowned."

Those other places were riddled with monsters as well, but he referred to them as if they were peaceful plains. It was hard to comprehend, even if it made sense that people like Billy and Cedric, who had surpassed normal human limitations, would struggle more with the elements than with monsters.

"All for the better. It doesn't feel quite right to raise my sword against those unfortunate beings, to be honest. It'd be easier if they were humans."

"Right. Let's take it and leave."

"All right."

Cedric slowly reached out his hand. His movement was cautious and hesitant, unlike the simple and determined answer he had given Billy. But in the end, his fingers closed firmly around the ruby.

The guardian stone offered no resistance as Cedric drew it toward him, even while it continued to maintain the eastern ward. The other stones hadn't resisted either, as if recognizing that their time had come. According to legend, they should have offered far more resistance. Their lack of opposition suggested that Cedric had the right—the right to possess them.

Even with all this power, Cedric had no ambition to do anything with it. Just the opposite, in fact. He felt like the stones acknowledged and approved of this. It was as if they were telling him that he wasn't wrong for doing this, that he was justified. It was why Cedric kept going, even as he hesitated, nursing one insignificant yet difficult wish in his heart.

Cedric clenched his fingers around the stone.

Crack!

With a resounding crack, the ruby crumbled into pieces. Its light faded.

Cedric picked out a small shard of the stone that was still glowing. As he looked into the ruby shard, he recalled a pair of eyes that had shone as brightly—no, even brighter.

"Brother! Cedric!"

He sighed. *The person I can never see again. The person I miss so dearly...*

"Sina, my lovely sister."

You.

It was the middle of the night, and everyone was asleep. Only when all sounds had ceased and the world was engulfed in darkness did Eid open his eyes.

He was slumped on the couch, unable to sleep though he wished he could. His eyes were empty, reflecting nothing. He was waiting—waiting for it all to finally end.

"Sina."

Because he despised these sleepless nights. He wanted these nights to stop existing altogether.

I'm sure you would hate to see me like this. You should have stayed with me, then.

CHAPTER
SIXTY

"Dummy."

"I know."

But that's how much I miss you.

"Go to sleep."

"If only I could."

He meant it. Eid wished he could fall into a deep sleep. He was exhausted, but he wanted to see her again, even if it was only in a dream. He'd hoped that tiring himself out would eventually allow him to fall asleep, but his exhaustion only piled up, and he still couldn't sleep. As if he wasn't allowed to.

"I wish everything would end soon." If it were going to fall anyway, he wished it would happen quickly. As soon as possible.

So that I can be with you.

He wanted to await their reunion with a joyful heart, but he was anxious. The more he remembered...

"Eid!"

...the less she showed herself.

But it wasn't all bad. As his mind wandered amid the haze of exhaustion, he still caught glimpses of her every now and then. *I want more.*

"Do you love me?"

A little more.

"Is that even a question?"

At the sound of her voice, which couldn't possibly be real, Eid quickly closed his eyes, making a wish to the moon that he could join her soon. He looked happy.

It was a beautiful night.

"Sir Yuri, a tsunami! There's been an urgent report that half the East has been flooded by a tsunami."

"All the ships have been partially damaged, affecting all exports."

"The surrounding countries have noticed the delay and are asking what is happening."

"Hersen is asking to be reimbursed, Sir Yuri."

Yuri sat absorbed as one drastic report after another assailed him without pause. He'd spent a wonderful evening the day before, after finally being able to go home for once. He'd taken a relaxing bath and had a wonderful night's sleep without worrying about work. While his bed at home might not have been as luxurious as the one provided for him at the palace, the fact that it was away from his workplace made it all the more comfortable.

He wondered whether he was being punished for having such a wonderful night. The gods didn't spare anyone.

"Maybe I should retire," he mused.

His subordinates, overhearing his mutterings even as they made their reports, gasped in horror, and clung to his sleeve.

"You mustn't!"

"You can't leave us like this."

"If you go, we're leaving with you."

It was utter chaos. There were tears in their eyes, making the scene even more dramatic.

Yuri's personal secretary, dead tired and uninterested in fueling this fire, pinched the bridge of his nose and ended the drama. "His Imperial Majesty won't approve it. Don't worry and keep working."

"Oh, right."

"True."

The situation instantly came to a close. They went back to their seats as if they hadn't been shedding tears.

Yuri felt his blood pressure rise as his subordinates suddenly stopped expressing any care for him. "So now the East has been affected?"

"Yes. The only region still untouched is the South."

"I suppose we should be thankful. Maybe it would have been better if things had started off in the South."

"Why is that?"

"That's where Grande lies."

"Even Grande won't be able to—"

"Shea may not be doing much to take care of the territory, but her ability to rule is incredible. She relies on her instincts, but those instincts are amazing, and she's a genius who always got top scores at Wordwith's. Her intelligence itself is far beyond average."

"Oh." The official nodded. Although he hadn't been at the academy at the same time as Shea, he knew how legendary she was. But that didn't justify everything. "But still, if we needed Shea Grande to take care of things, the other regions wouldn't have ended up like this."

"That's true," Yuri said, "but Grande has numerous brilliant minds and gifted individuals who would die for Shea Grande. That makes the South different from the other regions. If Grande were part of the empire's breadbasket, they would've saved at least part of the harvest, unlike the

West. Even without Shea ordering them around, everyone in Grande acts and works for her."

"Oh."

The difference between total annihilation and preserving a part of the harvest didn't seem like much, but those who worked to administer to the empire knew what a huge difference that would make. Saving one field might not save many people, but it would mean there were more alternatives coming.

"The whole empire is panicking because of this," Yuri said. "Even the capital, which hasn't been directly affected yet, is in chaos. The South may have been spared so far, but there's no way they haven't been affected in some way. And they know they'll be next. How is the South doing?"

"Now that you mention it..."

"The South operates around the Grande territory, so as long as Grande stands strong, the South stands strong as well. Grande may be refusing entry to more settlers now after taking in so many residents these past years, but that's it. They aren't having issues yet. I hear countless people are trying to move to Grande because of this. They're camping outside the borders, even though Grande has announced they wouldn't accept anybody."

"Isn't that a problem in itself?"

"It's a problem they've always had, since Grande has always been selective about new residents," Yuri said. "There's no use. People have always tried camping by the borders in protest. Grande was never kind to the rest of the empire. They'll scoff and say it's their own fault if people make a fuss and get themselves killed outside their borders, that it's their own fault for not leaving even after being warned. There are quite a few idiots who blame Grande, though."

"How pathetic. Why would they do such a thing? They know what Shea Grande is like."

"How many people do you think are aware that she rules the territory? That's why they're acting like fools. Not that she would give them the time of day."

"Oh, so that's what that was."

"Hmm?" Yuri asked. "What are you talking about?"

The man rummaged through his piles of paperwork and fished out a single piece of paper. "This. It's a message from Grande. It says that Grande is doing fine and wants to be left alone. In summary, they're telling us that they have enough on their hands taking care of their own territory, so we shouldn't shift blame or start anything we can't manage ourselves."

The message itself wasn't much longer than that.

Yuri clucked his tongue, shaking his head at how those under Shea acted like her. "In any case, we should be glad at least one region is doing well. We should be grateful that we have one less thing to worry about while we're already buried in work."

"That's true."

"Let's mind our own business and get back to work. Whew." Yuri let out a deep sigh as he glanced around the office, which contained so much paperwork that it was hard to spot the people working among the many piles. It was like a part of hell where the work was never-ending, no matter how hard he tried to get ahead of it. The scene before him sapped his motivation before he'd even begun.

"This is the schedule for the Glorious Assembly." His secretary destroyed the rest of his motivation on the spot.

"Maybe I really should retire."

Yuri Menthier had never been so desperate to end his career.

Meanwhile, as pandemonium engulfed everyone else, Edward slowly opened his eyes, feeling more comfortable and happier than he had in a long while. It was a truly wonderful morning.

Because Shea was by his side.

Just the fact that they were sharing each other's warmth made everything else irrelevant. It was a strange feeling, but even that made Edward happy. He wouldn't mind staying like this forever.

Overwhelmed by this contentment, he hugged Shea tightly and buried his face against her chest.

"Mm."

Shea struggled slightly in her sleep, but ended up with her arm wrapped around Edward, hugging him back. Whenever she did this, whether it was out of habit or because she could tell it was him, Edward was overwhelmed by pure bliss. It was a sense of joyous contentment that came with knowing he was the only one who could enjoy this side of her. Though he knew it wasn't entirely healthy, he found himself addicted to this feeling, so he tended to get up earlier than Shea to revel in her warmth. It was as if he was reaffirming her love for him.

Shea would have thought it was idiotic.

But Edward didn't care—because this was a luxury granted only to him. There was plenty of time left until she got up, and though he'd have to get to work eventually, it was all right to revel in this quiet moment a little longer. He'd worked so much overtime that this much should be allowed.

But then the communication device went off: Eid Roux Vencroft.

"What is it?" Edward asked.

"Get over here this instant."

What in the world did I ever do to you? "Is there even anything left that could go wrong at this point?"

"The pope's attendance at the Glorious Assembly has been accepted."

What? "Accepted by whom?"

"By the one hosting the assembly."

"Isn't the assembly tomorrow?"

"They waited this long on purpose to make everyone sweat. Get to work. We now have far more work to do before tomorrow."

Roux isn't real. If he were real, he couldn't possibly be this cruel to me.

Edward looked down at Shea's sleeping form. The sight of her asleep in her disheveled state—courtesy of himself—was otherworldly. He'd never seen anything so beautiful; it made his heart race. If he could just stand there and soak in this sight for the rest of his life, he would need nothing more.

And that was when he realized that he really had to leave, even though he didn't want to leave her. Because he wanted to keep seeing her.

"Get ready," he said into the device, gritting his teeth. "I'll be there shortly."

Eid turned off his end of the communication device without another word.

CHAPTER
SIXTY-ONE

"Ha."

Edward tried to dissipate his anger at the heartless way his friend had hung up on him. He needed to get moving, but tearing himself away was difficult. Unable to bring himself to get up, he stared down at Shea, who sensed his gaze and blearily opened her eyes.

Shea was so used to his staring that she simply rubbed her eyes. "Mm. Are you going to work?"

Edward smiled at how adorable she looked all sleepy like this, but his expression darkened as he realized he wouldn't see her again for much too long. He revealed the secret information as if it were nothing. "I need to attend the Glorious Assembly. I have to get going right away."

Glorious.

"The Glorious Assembly?" Her eyes widened as she repeated the words.

Edward pressed his lips against her temple and continued to spill national secrets, speaking as if it was nothing. "It'll be held tomorrow. Usually the imperial family, the prime minister, and founding members of the empire are invited, but attendance isn't required. I wasn't going to go, but now I've been roped into it."

"So, you're leaving now?"

"I have to. I have to go and join them immediately."

Shea bit her lip hesitantly, as if she had something to say.

Edward tilted his head in surprise. He'd expected her to disinterestedly tell him to have a good trip.

Faced with his questioning gaze, Shea was caught in a dilemma. *Should I tell him?* But she didn't have the right to spill such secrets. It wasn't enforced because it was an implied rule, but she had no idea what harm might come to her—or more specifically, to him—if she broke her silence.

All she could do was offer some lame advice. "Take some tranquilizers with you."

"Tranquilizers?"

"Something to help you calm down. Who knows what might happen there?"

He chuckled, thinking that she was poking fun at him, and showered her face with kisses. "I'll be back soon, Shea."

For you. That's what he seemed to imply as he said his goodbyes and made his way out.

She saw him off, waving calmly, waiting until she could no longer hear his footsteps to express her real feelings.

"Ugh." *Nothing ever goes my way.* She pulled at her hair in frustration and cursed her life for being so complicated. A few strands of hair floated to the floor, but she didn't care. "This is such a mess. What if I don't go?"

Although she didn't typically fulfill her obligations, attending the Glorious Assembly was the one duty she couldn't ignore. She felt like quitting. Nothing good would come from him finding out.

She rolled around on the bed for a long while before deciding to rise above it all. "He might faint. Well, that'll be a sight to behold."

An empty chuckle escaped her lips.

It was one day before the Glorious Assembly.

The meeting place for the Glorious Assembly was sacred ground, a place that nullified any supernatural powers, like the guardian stones that protected Vencroft. It was a sacred place that appeared to have been made by a god.

The meeting place couldn't be seen by the naked eye. Everyone knew its approximate location, but not exactly where it was. Only those with the right to enter could find it by arriving somewhere nearby and then walking on foot, which meant that they couldn't be joined by their attendants. It was as if to prove that all participants were equal.

"You must walk the rest of the way."

Most nobles were displeased with the lack of hierarchy, but those present today thought differently upon hearing about it.

Edward wanted it to end quickly so he could leave, but he was puzzled by a strange feeling of nostalgia.

Eid had to force his wildly beating heart to calm down. A strange, ridiculous feeling overcame him, a feeling that he might be able to meet someone he longed for.

Ace, who was there as the emperor's secretary and a representative of the Maxwell family, gritted his teeth and forced his buckling knees to support him. He felt as though he was about to face his past sins, and this was his atonement.

Last, Prime Minister Marquess Halbert Zestia, who was currently on leave of absence, closed his eyes at the thought that the truth he had hidden was about to be exposed. Though he hadn't ordered it to happen, Halbert had retired after hiding what had happened before he'd had a chance to intervene. He didn't have the audacity to act as though nothing had happened. He was cruel enough when she was alive. He couldn't bear to be cruel even after her death.

"Prime Minister?"

Halbert blinked at the sound of Eid's voice and turned to look at him: the man he'd watched grow up. The man he'd made emperor.

The embodiment of his indelible sins and resentment.

"You seem to be getting old," Eid said. "I've never seen you space out like that."

"It's been some time since I've been old. Now I simply wait for the end to come."

And with that, Halbert knew that he would finally be able to rest in peace today. He hadn't been able to kill himself because he knew he didn't have the right. He needed to be there to face the fury he'd forgotten against his wishes. He was genuinely happy at the thought that the day had finally come.

The person he blamed and placed his sins on would've laughed at him, saying that he still didn't know his place.

"Shall we, Your Imperial Majesty?" he said.

But he was still glad. And he hoped his death would help the emperor, if even a little.

As Halbert Zestia followed the emperor's lead, Ace followed the two of them, thinking very much the same. He'd committed the same sin. He was both relieved and racked with guilt at the thought of his sins finally being exposed, and he wondered whether this was what she would have wanted.

Each wrestling with their own hearts, they arrived at the Glorious meeting place, which exceeded their expectations. It resembled a court of law. The overwhelming sense of sacredness and grandeur left everyone wide-eyed and speechless.

A fairy appeared before them in a flash of light. "Welcome to the Glorious Assembly. My name is Lilith, and I have been given the role of mediator for this assembly. Please follow these lights. They will guide you to your seats."

"Are you a fairy?"

"Yes. I am a servant of the Great God Roux. I hope that this will be an enlightening day for you." Leaving behind these ominous words, she disappeared in another flash of light.

It seemed as though she would reappear once the assembly began, so they followed the small lights and sat down on the seats that appeared for them. There were only nine seats in the top row of the circular meeting place. The nobles took their seats below this row. They knew that this was to show that they were beneath those who would be seated above them. No one said a word—because they already knew who would be seated there.

They grew curious as to which seat belonged to whom. The old chairs were somehow ageless and sacred.

The people they didn't wish were here arrived.

"The pope is here."

"It looks like they only allowed three high priests to accompany him."

"The person in the middle must be the one who called for this assembly," said Halbert Zestia.

The pope and his high priests followed the fairy lights to their seats, and Verdel took his place at the center. The place for the host.

The fairy appeared in the middle of the circle and declared, "With the arrival of the host, I now declare that the Glorious Assembly has begun. Divine power can now be used, allowing the Children of God to enter this place. Dear guests, please be seated and prepare for the impact."

"The impact?"

The humans gathered here weren't ordinary people. Most magic shockwaves didn't affect them one bit. This also applied to those who served the god, even though they used magic instead of the holy powers they were never blessed with. They were also wearing plenty of shield artifacts, so there wasn't much of a difference between their defensive powers and those of the nobles.

So, this statement from the fairy made little sense to them.

But as soon as a light appeared in the top row, they understood what the fairy had meant. Even though it was only a flash of light, they found themselves momentarily unable to breathe.

"Ugh."

"I can't... breathe..."

"This is overwhelming."

A man appeared along with the flash of light. He sat down, as if he didn't see the people writhing in pain below him.

"Dean Byron of Peace, the eighth child, has arrived," Lilith announced.

Her voice was loud and clear, but none of the people in the lower rows could listen. They were busy dealing with the overwhelming pressure of several more flashes of light.

"Letis of Purification, the fourth child, has arrived."

"Ardel of Truth, the tenth child, has arrived."

"Rose Feira of Rage, the sixth child, has arrived."

Finally adjusting to the overwhelming power, the others could now observe the individuals appearing in their seats, in all their glory.

"Rowell of Restraint, the third child, has arrived."

They appeared to be adjusting their holy powers as soon as a new arrival appeared, though they couldn't help the arrival shockwaves. Now everyone was able to see every Child of God as they appeared.

CHAPTER SIXTY-TWO

"Ruperto of Memory, the fifth child, has arrived."

Their hair color, eye color, and even clothes were unique as they appeared, but as soon as they sat down, their hair turned platinum blond and their eyes turned blue, as if to show they'd been chosen by Roux. Their clothes changed into white robes, woven with divine power.

"Humans are certainly no match for them."

"Seeing them in person, I realize now that the insane emperor really was out of his mind for provoking them." Never mind the curse—the fact that anyone could act that way in front of such divine creatures was incomprehensible to Ace, whose comment might be considered slander against the imperial family.

But no one objected—because they all agreed. Edward agreed as well and turned to look at the Children of God once more.

It was hard to see them as being on the same level as humans, so what Ace said made perfect sense. They appeared to be untouchable and divine, like sacred creatures you weren't allowed to touch, no matter what. But even so, Edward couldn't help but think that their platinum-blond hair and blue eyes reminded him of Shea. He couldn't believe he was thinking about her, even as he was faced with these divine individuals. He smiled to himself, both exasperated and satisfied.

Someone very familiar appeared.

"Noise of Freedom, the second child, has arrived."

"Did she say—"

Noise. The name seemed too familiar. Edward had heard it not too long ago. He'd only heard it once, but because it was from Shea, he remembered it clearly. He could remember even the most banal of her comments.

Edward stared at the man, who sat down indifferently as his clothes, hair, and eye color changed. His face did indeed look familiar. As Edward's expression hardened with realization, Noise's eyes settled on him. Noise grinned down at him, and Edward met his gaze with a menacing glare, as if he were glad to see him.

Noise had basically confirmed his suspicions.

Edward narrowed his eyes at him. He didn't know what Noise was after, but he was prepared to fight anyone who might threaten Shea.

Noise chuckled, as if he were infinitely amused by Edward's attitude.

Edward didn't understand why Noise was laughing, but his heart sank.

There was another flash of light. Edward had no interest in tearing his eyes away from Noise, but Noise wiggled his eyebrows and signaled to him: *"Look over there."*

Though he didn't intend to indulge Noise, Edward found himself looking. His eyes grew wide. The person who appeared was a beautiful woman. She looked like the woman he loved. Her hair and eye color stayed the same as she sat down. Only her clothes turned to white robes.

He couldn't believe his eyes when the woman sat down and slowly opened her eyes.

"Shea?"

There was no doubt about it. Edward would have recognized that face, which he wanted to stare at all day, anywhere.

Having sensed his gaze on her, Shea looked down at him and smiled. It was mesmerizing.

Lilith announced her arrival. "Lariana of Life, the seventh child, has arrived."

The whole meeting place erupted with exclamations of shock. Anyone who lived in the capital of Vencroft was familiar with her face.

"That face!"

"Shea Grande!"

"But her eyes and hair color haven't changed!"

"That's because they were always that color."

"Edward van Griffith."

"Shea Grande? Is that really her?" Caught completely off guard, Ace couldn't help raising his voice in surprise, asking Edward to confirm it. *Is that really her?*

But Edward was unable to answer. He was having a hard time grasping what was happening.

Eid struggled, too, though he'd always thought she was extraordinary. He stared in confusion, having never expected this.

There was only one person who wasn't surprised by Shea's presence: Halbert Zestia. He looked up at her, his eyes full of remorse, guilt, and reverence.

Shea gave him a mocking smile, as if to say it was too little, too late.

A flash of light on the middle seat drew the attention of the Children of God. As an elderly man appeared in its place, they rose to their feet and respectfully greeted him.

Lilith sounded reverent as she announced his arrival. "Solomon of Wisdom, the first child, has arrived."

It was then that the Children of God spoke for the first time.

"Our undying respect to the first of all knowledge."

"Our respect to the meaningless curse of immortality."

"Wait, isn't that an insult?"

"Well, it's true."

"You can't help yourself, can you?"

The humans were flabbergasted by their casual tone, but the Children of God ignored them as they talked among themselves.

Solomon smiled a fatherly smile as he watched the other Children of God squabble. "I see you haven't changed."

"It wouldn't be like us to change. We won't change a bit, as long as we live."

"For your sake, at least."

Shea spoke up along with the others. "Our respect to you, who came before us and will remain after we are gone."

Edward squeezed his eyes shut at the sound of Shea's unmistakable voice. He didn't feel betrayed that she had kept this secret; he understood the unwritten law that Children of God must not reveal their identities, even to their loved ones. Besides, she was still Shea, even as a Child of God.

But he was shaken by this revelation because of the weight she must've been carrying on her shoulders, as a Child of God. He couldn't imagine how heavy that burden must have been—all those secrets a Child of God would have to keep.

And Shea had endured it on her own. He'd had no idea, concerned only with enjoying her attention. He couldn't raise his head out of shame for having been such a fool.

Shea, who seemed to understand what was going through Edward's mind, let out a few huffs of exasperated laughter and burst into chuckles. Her smile was lovely.

The other Children of God eyed her mischievously and began to tease her. "Wow, you didn't tell your boyfriend beforehand? He looks like he's about to faint."

"You should've told him—if you were going to see him here. Look at him—he's wilting away."

"It's true that your identity is a private matter best kept secret... but look at the poor man."

Shea put a stop to everyone's meddling comments with a sharp snap. "Shut up. Stop meddling in my business. And he's still adorable, so it's fine."

Edward, who felt like he wanted to start digging a hole in the ground to hide, quickly looked up. She gave him a cheerful smile, her eyes full of affection, and he felt like crying. He no longer cared about anything else. She was his world, and he was over the moon about it.

The other Children of God, bothered by the heart-eyes they were making at each other, pushed Lilith to start the assembly.

"Ugh, I'm starting to get annoyed. Let's stop."

"Right? Hurry up, Lilith."

"I don't want to see public displays of affection."

Shea rolled her eyes at the others' antics. They hadn't changed. "Go ahead, Lilith."

Everyone nodded.

"Understood," Lilith said. "The Glorious Assembly will now commence. Everything that is said from now on will be sent to the Great God Roux, and whatever is discussed here may affect the future of this world. Let us begin with Verdel Isis Hydia, the ninth child, who called for this assembly. Isis of Indulgence, please announce the topic of discussion for this assembly."

Verdel rose from his seat. "As you know, three of the four guardian stones protecting Vencroft have been destroyed. Repairing these is—"

"Nonsense, yes."

"Yes. None of you here, even if you had the ability to do so, have any intention of repairing them."

No one raised an objection to this almost rude statement of fact, not one of the nine Children of God. Even though they'd been blessed with special powers. Even though so many sacrifices had been made to sustain Vencroft.

Ace gritted his teeth. He knew he shouldn't. Having been saddled with duty in exchange for gaining power as a noble, he knew how awful it was to be roped into a duty you hadn't wished for. He was also well aware that the Children of God had no reason to use their powers for humans.

But if things came to an end like this, then those sacrifices would become meaningless. So even though he knew he shouldn't, Ace spoke up. "But why?"

"Ace?" It was uncharacteristic of Eid to look so shocked, but Ace was the last person he expected to butt in.

Even with Eid staring at him, Ace found himself unable to stop. "All of you have power. This is a matter of life and death for hundreds, if not thousands, of citizens. If not for situations like this, what are your powers for? Blood has been spilled countless times to protect it. Those sacrifices can't just—in any case, you *can* help."

Oh, no. I did it. Despite being stunned by his own recklessness, Ace felt better at getting it off his chest. He wanted to be unreasonable and let it all out, because he'd never been able to do so before. He hadn't been able to cry when he wanted to because he didn't deserve to.

"Negative emotions only distract from the topic at hand," began Lilith. "If this happens again—"

"It's fine, Lilith." Rose Feira, the Child of Rage, turned to look down at Ace.

CHAPTER
SIXTY-THREE

The look in Rose Feira's eyes was so cold that it was easy to see why her title was "of Rage."

"What you've said is only natural for a human to feel," she said. "After all, it is human nature to be willing to sacrifice someone else for your own gain, even if you know it to be wrong. As you said, Vencroft has been built on and sustained by countless sacrifices. At its founding, one of us sacrificed himself for the empire, and that empire has continually shed blood and sacrificed more people because it could not be satisfied with the blessing it did not deserve."

"..."

"You ignore the fact that this cannot go on forever and that your empire has enjoyed many more luxuries than any other nation. And yet, that is not enough?"

"..."

"That reckless shamelessness has merely reached its limit now. So why should we interfere?"

Ace raised his voice. "That's—"

"Who are you to deserve our help? What makes you more special than those from other nations?" she retorted coldly.

None of the humans, including Ace, could respond to her chilling fury. Although no one said anything, they shared the same hope as Ace. In the end, it was human nature to hope.

Except for one, the only remaining member of the Vencroft bloodline. Shea's lips parted slowly, and she gazed into Eid's empty eyes. "Ace Maxwell."

"...!"

"The changes currently going on in the empire are a result of the world returning to its natural state, after having been artificially enhanced by the guardian stones all these years. Though harm has been done, no human life has been lost. Is it not so?"

Ace nodded. "You are correct."

It was just as Shea said. Though there had been a cold front in the North, a bad harvest in the West, and a tsunami in the East, the disasters had affected only properties and assets. No human life had been lost, not even one.

"As you said, the history of Vencroft is one of sacrifices," she continued. "First, through our blood, and thereafter, through the blood of the Vencroft imperial family."

"...!"

"The truth has been entrusted to the Maxwell family for generations. You must have seen it happen, as well. I have a question for you. You, who know the empire's entire history, as the successor of the Maxwell family."

"..."

"In order to maintain something that has barely persisted through countless sacrifices, another sacrifice is necessary," she said. "Is that what you desire? Who and what would that sacrifice benefit?"

"I-I..." Ace looked around at Eid in shock.

It was just as she said. Among all the founding families, the Maxwells were the closest to the imperial family, having served them loyally for generations. As such, the Maxwell family was entrusted with the secrets of both the imperial family and the empire.

The men of the Maxwell family were honest and true. They reminded their descendants not to make the same mistakes and never to forget the sacrifices that had been made. Ace knew all these secrets.

Yet before him was the emperor, who had sacrificed something enormous without his knowledge.

Ace found himself at a loss for words.

"Let's proceed." Shea signaled for things to continue when Ace finally hung his head, as if she didn't care how he was feeling.

But the other Children of God didn't seem to care either. Since they experienced emotions differently from humans, this was only natural except for Verdel, who may have been harder on humans than the other Children of God but had stooped so low as to be on level with Ace.

Verdel thought that it was good that Vencroft, who had been deceived, betrayed, and reduced to shreds countless times without his knowledge, had someone like Ace by his side. Yet Verdel was about to do something even more cruel to him.

"The discussion will continue," Shea said. "Isis."

"Understood," Verdel said. "I shall continue. As everyone has said, Vencroft is currently in chaos because the guardian stones have been broken and nature is returning to its original state. If the emperor pays the price, the empire's blessing may persist a while longer. But the current emperor has already paid a price. He is the last of his line."

Shea furrowed her eyebrows at his ominous tone and cut in. "You're rambling. Get to the point."

"I would like to hear the opinions of those who could bring change to Vencroft. Though the current emperor is known to have no children, Eid Roux Vencroft has one successor who has been erased from his fate."

"...!"

Eid's eyes widened.

Ace, who had been cowering, also appeared to be in shock.

Halbert Zestia squeezed his eyes shut. He wasn't brave enough to look his emperor in the eye.

Verdel continued steadily, "We must decide whether to place Elias Grande, son of Eid Roux Vencroft and Sistina Illid Vencroft, next in line for the throne, thereby receiving another blessing to sustain the empire, even if the last guardian stone is destroyed and the blessing weakens"—he paused to draw a breath—"or whether to stand by and watch as Vencroft crumbles. Like it or not, we have been with Vencroft since its founding days. I called this meeting because we need to discuss our course of action regarding the potential fall of the empire."

"…"

Those who were faced with the unexpected truth were rendered speechless with shock.

Shea kept quiet even as Verdel handed her this death sentence. The other Children of God clucked their tongues in cxasperation.

"He's insane, just insane."

"Really? You're provoking Lariana of all people, Isis? You couldn't possibly be stupid enough to mess with Life, could—wait, yes, you could. Forget what I said."

"He keeps digging his own grave, even though we keep warning him."

"Let him dig it and suffer. I don't care."

"I wondered what he was going to bring up, with this pomp and grandeur."

"Why did you even call us here? What nonsense."

"Why did father even allow this? Has he finally gone crazy from boredom?"

"Hey, he's always been crazy."

"Oh, right. My mistake."

The shocking truth became nothing but dust in the wind. It didn't matter to them. They'd lived through a lot and heard a lot of things, and there was no way they hadn't known about the change in fate. They'd covered it up, as fate demanded. Not one of them had ever thought to change that fate, because everyone had been in Verdel's position before. And after going through it, they realized something.

It was meaningless. You simply had to endure it.

But Verdel, born with Indulgence, was proud until the end and refused to let it go. Like a fool.

Eid wasn't listening as the Children of God sighed and groaned around him. There was only one name that echoed in his ears: Sistina Illid Vencroft.

Only an empress could hold the name Vencroft. A mere mistress had no right to that supposedly glorious name. And yet, she was called by that name.

Eid had never liked his name, but at this very moment, he couldn't have been more thrilled about it, because it proved she had actually been his. Because there was something left of her, even though she was gone.

He thought he might cry.

We have a child. A piece of evidence that we were together.

Sina. We really were together. I thought there was nothing left, but you left something behind for me.

"Ha! Haha."

As Eid's eyes reddened, Ace saw that Eid was happy, horrifyingly happy.

Ace shut his eyes. He'd thought the child had disappeared along with her. He'd forgotten about it, and yet the child had survived. He hated himself for feeling relieved. He didn't deserve to feel like that.

The pope proclaimed his tactless opinion, his nose in the air. "We must put the boy on the throne, of course. The blessing of Vencroft is greater whenever a new emperor takes the throne. With that blessing, we will be able to sustain the empire even if the last guardian stone is destroyed."

"Roux would never send us a disaster we cannot handle," one of his priests agreed. "This, too, is Roux' will."

"Indeed," noted another. "Roux always puts us first. Clearly, he has prepared this solution for us."

The sight of the priests and the pope chattering about what Roux was like in the presence of the Children of God themselves was laughable. Even the fairy who was there to be an impartial mediator and record the proceedings scoffed.

But the pope's opinion was still an opinion. As long as that opinion was stated during the proceedings, it had to be respected, according to the rules of the Glorious Assembly.

The first Child of God, Solomon of Wisdom, spoke up. "The blessing of Vencroft is changed out whenever someone blessed by Roux is put on the throne. In the end, it is more like an exchange of blessings than an addition. For a new blessing to be received, the one receiving it must succeed the throne. If Elias Grande becomes the successor, does the empire then plan to put a four-year-old child on the throne?"

While those from the imperial palace should have been the ones to answer, the pope shamelessly raised his voice. "Of course. There has already been a precedent of a four-year-old on the throne in Vencroft. Both his mother and other members of the imperial family, as well as the aristocracy, took on their share of duties to support him, but that will also be possible in this case if the temple helps out."

"..."

Everyone looked at him in disgust, tutting at him. It was clear that he intended to sit by and watch as everyone else did the work. It was almost impressive to see someone so consumed by their own greed, even in such a grave situation as this.

Shea, who'd been keeping quiet even though this concerned her own son, slowly parted her lips to speak.

CHAPTER
SIXTY-FOUR

Shea gave the pope an ominous smile, as though curious about how someone could be so brave. "So, are you saying you will sacrifice my son? You dare to say this in front of me?"

Her words were so menacing that it felt like she was about to decapitate anyone who agreed to sacrifice her son.

The pope hesitated at her frightening tone but soon opened his mouth again, confident as someone who raked in a lot of money through his way with words. "What sacrifice? I mean to bestow upon him the highest seat in the empire. How could anyone come to such a negative conclusion, when all we want is to give him everything he could possibly want?"

Shea let out a scoff of exasperation at the flattery that flowed from his tongue like slippery oil. "It's obvious you intend to have everything for yourself by manipulating the boy and making him your puppet. You're a smooth talker."

Everyone held their breath at her chilling response. Bloodshed was prohibited during the assembly, but everyone who knew Shea knew that she did whatever she put her mind to.

Dean Byron, the Child of God who loved peace, prayed to Roux that he wouldn't see any bloodshed today, or at least that Shea would deal with that man out of sight. His hopes, however, were dashed.

"Once Elias takes on the name of Vencroft," Shea continued, "he will inherit the Vencroft curse, as he becomes the successor. He is currently not affected by it because I removed him from the family line and gave him my own name. And yet, you still wish for this to happen?"

"That is a reasonable—"

"It's all the same to you since you won't be the one affected, huh? Does this seem like a suitable place for your garbage opinions?"

"…!"

Shea had run out of patience. She'd made up her mind while he spouted nonsense, treating everyone as though they were beneath him. He wasn't worth anything.

The pope felt weighed down by the disgust in her eyes; he was no longer even human to her.

Noticing the pope's anguish, Lilith tried to deter Shea. "Lariana, this is a Glorious Assembly. Please suppress your powers."

But Shea didn't listen to Lilith, not even one bit. "Lily, you seem to be deluding yourself because we're being polite. Do you want to cease existing? You should remember who it is you're talking to. As you know, I'm not a very gracious person."

Slam!

"...!"

Lilith suddenly crashed into the ground, forced her head up against the impossible force that pushed her down, and gazed up at Shea—the beautiful, chillingly emotionless woman who hadn't moved even a finger to slam her into the ground. Shea was usually indifferent, and Lilith hadn't seen her in so long that she'd been careless. She had forgotten that Shea was the only person here who wouldn't be stopped even if she killed Lilith, the woman who had all the love of Roux.

Fear flitted across Lilith's face for the first time.

"That's enough, Lariana," Solomon said. "Lilith may have overstepped her place, but your warning is going too far."

Shea's reply sounded nonchalant. "I didn't really do anything."

"Lilith could die at a mere flick of your finger. Remember how powerful you are."

"All right. I suppose it's only polite to listen to my elder." She withdrew her powers.

Lilith let out a cough and sucked in a few hurried breaths, as the pressure holding her down finally dissipated. Once she'd caught her breath, she rose to her knees facing Shea. "P-please excuse my insolence. I shall always keep in mind who you are—until the day I die."

"You'd better. I don't really want to kill you."

Lilith bowed her head with a respect completely different from the politeness she'd shown so far.

Shea turned away. "My annoyance got the best of me. I seem to have changed the subject."

"..."

"You seem to be forgetting a fundamental fact: That boy is Elias Grande, not Elias Roux Vencroft. Therefore, he is *my* child, not the son of Eid Roux Vencroft."

"You cannot deny his bloodline!"

"Sure, I won't deny that."

As she unexpectedly relented, Eid's head shot up so he could look at her. Getting clear confirmation was different from suspecting something.

Shea ignored him. She had no interest in an emperor who couldn't even save the woman he loved. "It was difficult to end the Vencroft curse. Merely giving the boy my surname wasn't enough. Many members of the Vencroft family tried to escape the curse by changing their names, but it never worked for the same reason. The Vencroft blessing becomes meaningless unless the person ascending the throne carries the name."

"Does that mean the Vencroft blessing has been taken away from the crown prince?" Ace asked.

The Vencroft blessing was proof of belonging to the Vencroft bloodline, akin to being acknowledged by the Great God Roux himself. All members of the Vencroft family simultaneously received both their curse and blessing. There had been cases where an unchosen individual received only the curse, but none had received the blessing without also bearing the curse. Not even one.

"Good question. Yes and no."

"Pardon?"

"Obviously, I can't replace all the blood in his body. Fortunately, both of his parents were blessed, so it was easier for me. The curse relented a little, you see. It was actually because of his mother."

Shea thought of Sistina, the fool who hadn't changed even as she drew her last breath. Sistina remained unchanged even as she worked at the imperial palace. Shea couldn't find it in her to hate her. She would probably care for her forever. "Before Sistina Illid died, she left me a gift. She said she was giving me her most treasured possession.

That gift was Elias. But back then, I had no idea what she meant."

"Most treasured?" Eid said.

The exasperation Shea had felt that day rushed back as Eid repeated those words. Before closing her eyes for the last time, Sistina had told her many cryptic things that even she, the great Shea Grande, couldn't decipher. She'd been so confused. But because Sistina's death had been more important in that moment, she'd forgotten about her last words.

"Only when Halbert Zestia forced a newborn baby into my arms did I realize that the boy was the gift she had referred to," Shea said. "So, I demanded that he swear that this child would be mine and mine alone, if he were going to force me to keep it. And I demanded proof of the transaction."

"But that means—"

"Halbert Zestia."

Halbert slowly raised his head at the emperor's voice. As he looked into those cold eyes, full of fury and sorrow, the old man realized it was time for the truth. "Yes. I took Elias and gave him to Shea."

"But why?"

"Because it was her wish. I had never once paid any attention to my granddaughter, but I wanted to fulfill her last wish."

There was a collective gasp.

"…!"

"Sistina Illid was the daughter of my son, the late Marquess Illid."

Halbert Zestia had two sons. His second son was considerate and selfless, in stark contrast to his devious older brother, who preferred their father to retain his title as long as possible to avoid any responsibilities. The second son respected the Zestia name and cherished his freedom and leisure. So, when his wife passed away, Zestia bequeathed his wife's title and lands to his second son, who then left Zestia Manor to travel freely around the empire.

Halbert was proud of his son for living independently without being a burden, yet he also wished for him to settle down. Wanting to keep him close, he arranged a marriage for his son.

But then his son arrived with a woman he wanted to marry. She was simple, naive, and sweet, but not a noble—just a commoner, and an orphan at that. The Zestia March had no need to strengthen its position through marriage, yet Halbert found the match completely unacceptable. He sent her far away, making sure his son would never see her again, and forced his son into an arranged marriage.

That was how Cedric Illid was born, a boy conceived on the wedding night—with the aid of alcohol, at that.

Thankfully, the woman who became the son's wife did not love him. He appeared to give up and settle down when she became pregnant, but eventually he left everything to her and ran off to his true love. In the end, he found her and lived happily ever after, without a title and with no money, until they died on the same day.

Sistina was the proof of their happiness, but Halbert chose to ignore her. She was a reminder of his failings. If only he had made better choices, she wouldn't have been born out of wedlock. The sweet girl seemed to understand how he felt, because she never tried to get his attention. His heart ached, but he was glad that she didn't.

But one day, she came to see him, caressing her small baby bump. "If I die, please protect this child—and bring him to Shea. She'll recognize him. Please, grandfather."

It was her first and only request. He'd planned on ignoring it at first, but then she passed away. It was as if her request to him was a prediction.

In the end, Halbert couldn't refuse her last wish, even though he knew it would've been better to turn a blind eye. He wasn't that heartless.

CHAPTER
SIXTY-FIVE

Halbert Zestia's voice strengthened. "So, I gave Shea Grande the Seal of Arthur, just as she demanded."

"Prime Minister!" Forgetting where he was, Ace leaped to his feet.

Edward's eyes widened too.

Unlike the other founding families of the empire, the Zestia family had no power. All they had was their wisdom. To protect them, the first emperor bestowed the first Marquess Zestia with three seals imbued with divine power, giving the wielder the ability to make a divine declaration—the ultimate command, a declaration even the emperor couldn't refuse. Because of this, the Zestias' role became that of secretary to the imperial family, but with the power to correct and lead.

The Vencroft Empire had persisted for several centuries. Two of the seals had already been used. Only one was left.

And Halbert Zestia had just given the remaining seal away.

Shea clucked her tongue as if she were very much displeased. "This is why I don't like you, Halbert Zestia. That doesn't make up for what you did. Why didn't you treat her well while she was still alive?"

"I've lived in regret ever since," he replied. "I will repay the rest of my debt to her after I die."

"Do you think she'll be willing to see you in the afterlife?"

"I believe so. She had a kind heart."

"Sweet words from the man who killed her with neglect." After stabbing him in the heart with those cold words, she went back to the topic at hand. "In any case, I used the Seal of Arthur to change Elias' name from Vencroft to Grande. His mother had already given permission, so the seal was enough. So, the boy became my son. He is my son, not a crown prince for you to decide what to do with."

"..."

No one was able to object. They knew very well that nothing could change what had been declared in the words of Roux.

"Eid Roux Vencroft," she said.

"Shea Grande."

"Do you intend to take back your son? And if you could, could you really protect him—"

"That..."

"—when you couldn't even protect the woman you loved?"

Eid slumped forward, as if the strength had left his body. That was enough of an answer.

"If you need a Vencroft child that badly, make him have another one," she said. "It's not as if the curse guarantees that he will die early, and his bodily functions should be working fine even if he loses his mind. I have no interest in the fate of Vencroft. If it falls, it falls. The empire will come to an end eventually. It could be sooner or later. We simply watch as its fate comes to pass."

The other Children of God lost interest in the debate as soon as she delivered these firm words. It meant that they agreed with her. They were acting as if the matter was settled.

The pope, who'd been confident in his plan to use Elias, furrowed his eyebrows. "But—"

"No buts. My son will have no part in helping you desperately hold onto the things you can't bring yourself to let go of."

Solomon turned to Verdel as if to conclude the assembly. "Is that all you have to discuss, Verdel Isis Hydia?"

"..."

Verdel wordlessly looked at Shea.

She let out a huff of exasperated laughter. He was foolish until the very end.

The other Children of God gave him similarly derisive looks.

"How could you not learn a single thing from losing everything? It's astounding. Every one of us realized at least one thing."

"Right? Maybe it's because he's the brashest and youngest of us."

"I don't begrudge father for trying something new, but there's a reason he never did it again."

"Ardel came after him, and he isn't like that."

Turning away from the others' cruel, cold comments, Shea looked down at Verdel with pity at how pathetic humans could be. "You consider us to be 'whole.' Even when we keep telling you we're not, even now that you've wound up here after failing, you still think we're whole. I find that strange and astounding. Maybe your critical thinking skills are negligible."

"As if," he muttered.

"Do you really think I decided on my own to ignore you when you begged me to resurrect the woman you love?"

"What?" He blinked up at Shea, clearly unable to understand what she was saying or why she had suddenly changed the topic.

His reaction convinced her. *It never occurred to him.*

The other Children of God commented on his reaction.

"I'm downright jealous that you're able to think like that."

"I wish we could be like him."

"How annoying."

Shea agreed with them. It was impressive, how it had never occurred to him. "You are of Indulgence. The most you can do with your abilities is succeed in your little business endeavors. I suppose that's why you never experienced it. I envy you."

"Please say it in a way I can understand," Verdel requested, his voice low. His eyes were full of defiance, like those of a petulant child, and denial, as if he refused to recognize the truth.

The other Children of God exchanged glances, wondering who could explain this to him plainly.

In the end, the responsibility fell to Shea. "We are only halves, my child. You may not have felt this because you've only ever used your powers for trivial things. It wouldn't have affected you. Why wouldn't we use our powers willy-nilly, like you? It's not as if they run out."

"..."

"Using our powers to a certain degree is fine. But anything regarding matters on a grand scale or anything that greatly changes someone's fate is different. Things like bringing a loved one back to life, like you requested."

"...!"

"I am of Life. My power doesn't run out. What reason could there be for me to ignore your request when you came to me in such desperation? Because I have some sort of grudge against you? I find you foolish, but I never hated you. Why in the world would I have refused to fulfill your wish?"

Even though the answer was clear, Verdel took a long moment to contemplate it, as if he were looking for another reason because he refused to accept the one that was true. In the end, he had to give in. There was only one answer, no matter which way he tried to twist it. "Because you couldn't?"

"You're correct. It's not like our powers are without restrictions. My powers are more heavily restricted than others. Like you, I once failed and had to pay the price. Because of this, there's a clear boundary between the lives I can and can't save. I can't resurrect anyone whose return would alter the fate of someone significant."

"But I'm—she was a normal—"

"She was someone loved by fate. Because you loved her. That in itself made her someone I couldn't bring back to life. If she were to live, your fate would change."

"...!"

Verdel's jaw dropped in shock. He'd blamed others and himself, but he'd never blamed himself. He looked like a child in his state of shock.

Shea patiently told him the truth, as she had the day he awakened to his powers. "When she died, you came to me in tears and asked me why I didn't save her, when I had the power to do so. You asked why the rules were so important."

"I—"

"You are a foolish, foolish boy. Those rules exist not for humans but for our sake. Every one of us except you has lost something or been banned from something as a result of our failure. We made those rules for us, so we don't get hurt."

"..."

"I, too, have rules that I strictly follow. No matter who comes to me, even if I can, I will not bring anyone back to life." *How do you not know?* "I can't save everyone. They all die in the end. Letting things be is what life is about. What good will come from interfering in someone's life? They only come back to demand my help yet again, as if they're entitled to it, and resent me when I refuse."

"..."

"Just like you did."

"...!"

He was the only one who didn't know the thing that every Child of God knew instinctively, without needing it to be explained. It made him seem so much like a child, even though he was older than her. The Children of God technically counted their age from the moment they awakened to their powers.

How foolish and human of him.

Everyone knew that although the Children of God were technically human, their point of view was completely different. That's why they never interfered. Only one of them—only Verdel—was still as human as those without powers.

What a pity.

"I have the power to bring people back to me," Shea continued. "But even when my parents died, even when I lost a dear friend, I didn't bring any of them back to life. Who knows what twisting their fates would entail if I forced them back to life?"

"..."

"The same goes for the others. None of them came to me when their loved ones died. Except you. That was when I first realized you were different from the rest of us."

"Shea."

"Even though you awoke to your powers, you're still a mere human. I'm almost jealous of your ignorance and how you foolishly think of no one but yourself."

How nice it would have been to be as ignorant as you. She genuinely wished for it, because she'd found out, as a human who surpassed all others, how precious such ignorance was.

CHAPTER
SIXTY-SIX

Shea envied Verdel when he took her simple statement of the truth as an insult. It was upsetting how jealous of him she was.

"Even so," he cried, "I'd have done everything I could to bring her back to life. Even now, I would make that same decision. All you're doing is making your—our—idleness and avoidance sound reasonable!"

She didn't respond with anger, only a bitter smile. "That's why we keep saying you're a child."

Verdel wanted to shout at her and get angry for smiling like that, but he found himself unable to do so, even though his other siblings were looking at him with the same smile. Some unspecified emotion, something like anger or resentment, was taking hold of him.

Suddenly, the Children of God simultaneously widened their eyes as if in shock. A single tear rolled down each of their cheeks. The humans turned to look at them, confused by their sudden change in attitude.

Gold flecks of light floated down like snow.

The humans in attendance looked around, clueless and confused, as the Children of God wiped away their tears and mumbled their complaints.

"What a waste of time."

"This wasn't a debate. Maybe our job was to teach the immature kid a lesson."

"It doesn't look like he understood, though. The great Shea even deigned to explain it to him."

"She actually explained it nicely for once. Tsk."

Shea let out an exasperated laugh. "You're the ones who made me explain it! Why did you make me do it?"

"Because he only listens to you, even if only a little."

"He refuses to listen to our elder here because he says Solomon sounds like an old coot, but he remembers what you say. Maybe because you're of Life?"

"Did you read the truth again? Stop it, it's creepy."

Shea shuddered at the thought of the ability Truth being used. Nobody would be happy to have their inner thoughts revealed by someone else.

Ardel of Truth, who knew that his abilities weren't welcomed by anyone, still looked upset when Shea put it so plainly. "I can't read you, so don't worry, okay? When everyone was younger and didn't know how to use their abilities well, I could read them. But I can only read him now because his divine powers are nearly gone, so who cares?"

"I don't like it," Shea said. "My tongue is sore from talking so m—" *Cough!*

Everyone leaped to their feet when she coughed up blood in the middle of her sentence.

"...!"

"Lariana!"

"Shea!"

"Hey!"

"Are you okay?"

Edward's eyes reddened, so shocked that he was rendered speechless. His gaze wavered, and he looked unable to accept what was happening. In case something was wrong. In case he lost her—again.

It took so long to get you.

His mind filled with chaotic thoughts. Though he would've been confused by them even if he'd been in his right mind, he didn't realize how strange they were because the situation at hand had shaken him to the core.

No one understood what was happening to Edward except Shea, who treasured him above all. She tried to appear nonchalant as she wiped the blood from her lips, clenching her hand and striving to conceal its trembling. *Ugh, what a jerk. I didn't even say much, and he shut me up anyway.*

"Quiet down. It's nothing."

Her siblings shouted at her as soon as she spoke up.

"You coughed up blood! How is that nothing?"

"We never get sick, but you coughed up blood! How are we supposed to ignore that?"

She tutted amid everyone's concerns, seeing that they weren't thinking about why this might have happened. "We may not get sick, but *this* kind of thing happens to us sometimes. Remember?"

"What are you—oh."

"Yes, that," she said. "He seems displeased about my revealing so much. This is his twisted way of showing it."

How in the world can he be a god? She clucked her tongue and muttered to herself, and the other Children of God let out groans of recognition. They'd known about this, but this was new.

"Wow, how incredibly petty."

She smiled bitterly. "Right? Why did you make me explain? My body may be fine, but this doesn't feel good, you know."

"We knew you had more restrictions, as much as you're loved the most, but we didn't think it would be this bad."

"It *is* this bad," she said, "so don't make me do things like this anymore."

"We'll keep that in mind."

"I'll write it down."

"Don't do that." *Why would you record this for the next generation?*

When Ruperto of Memory piped up, Shea quickly dissuaded him. Unlike the other Children of God, Ruperto had a name that had been passed down for generations. Along with receiving his abilities, Ruperto also remembered everything that had happened since the first Ruperto. That's why the Ruperto of every generation wished for his life to be over soon. There was a rumor that Ruperto was the reason the Children of God had become unable to die until they were allowed to.

In any case, Shea had no desire to be recorded as an irregularity in his collective memory, and she hated being recorded.

Lilith began to explain what was happening to the humans, who had no idea what was going on. "The last guardian stone has been destroyed. The lights you saw were the residue of the ward disappearing. The wards that have protected Vencroft all these years are now gone. All land in the empire will now return to its natural state, as it was before the empire was founded. Just as the Children of God have commented already, this debate has become fruitless."

A buzz went around the meeting place as soon as Lilith finished speaking.

"...!"

"What?"

Eid looked relieved, as if he were happy it was over, and there was a mixture of relief and regret in Marquess Zestia's eyes. Edward wasn't interested in any of this.

The only ones going pale with dread at the thought of what would happen next were Ace and the priests.

The priests had been complicit in the destruction of the guardian stones. Their plan had been to leave the one in the South alone, because they knew that the luxuries they enjoyed would disappear if all four stones were destroyed. Their original plan had been to leave one ward intact and place a puppet under their control on the throne after putting pressure on the imperial palace. In order to inflict a sense of dread on the empire, they'd given up the West and chosen the South, with its great balance of trade and farming, to remain untouched.

But now the southern stone had been destroyed. They would have to recalculate their whole strategy. Their bargaining chip had now disappeared, and they were in a state of great emergency.

The pope ground his teeth in frustration. They knew that the man wasn't under their control, but they'd never expected him to make such a huge mistake. Their mistake had been to assume that he wouldn't be able to destroy all four stones, since he himself was a noble.

They needed to get back as quickly as possible to discuss this.

The pope got to his feet, trying to get Verdel's attention in a hurry.

A beam of light erupted in the middle of the meeting place, right in front of Verdel.

Whoosh!

"...!"

A single, translucent flower appeared with the beam of light. It almost looked like the manifestation of all divine energy, gathered in one place. Those who didn't know what this flower symbolized looked on in renewed confusion.

Verdel hurriedly grabbed it. His desperation was laughable, seeing that the flower was easily within his reach. He looked as though he'd been waiting for this.

The other Children of God realized the real reason Verdel had gathered them here today.

"Oh, so that's what he was after."

"When it's used up quickly, it appears wherever there is a conflation of divine energy. Wow, he used his brain for that one."

"We can't fully control our divine energy during a Glorious Assembly, after all."

Verdel hurriedly stowed away the flower. He looked anxious as he asked, "Are you going to take it from me?"

The Children of God gave him the same look as they replied simultaneously, "Why would we?"

He had imagined they might react this way, but he hadn't expected them to be so nonchalant. He stared in disbelief.

Shea let out a chuckle. "Why would we need that? You're the only one who does. You got to it first, so it's yours. Do with it as you wish."

"Even though you know what I'm going to do?"

She got to her feet. "I think everyone here knows. It's the coagulation of divine energy from someone long gone. It's not their soul or anything, so we have no reason to be bothered."

As she rose, the other Children of God also got up, no longer interested in what was happening.

Once every Child of God was standing upright, Solomon spoke. "It is up to you to decide what to do with it. Just as

Lariana said, do with it as you wish. We will not stop you. The only reason we participated in this Glorious Assembly today, even though there was little reason—"

"Solomon…"

"…is because of you. You, who still haven't given up, unlike the rest of us." Solomon looked down at Verdel with infinite benevolence.

The others looked down at Verdel in the same way, knowing what he was about to do, yet they seemed to respect his decision—as if they thought him foolish. But none of them would blame him or hate him.

"We hope that your future will be blessed," Solomon finished, "my foolish and lovely child."

Verdel hung his head at Solomon's kind voice; it was the only courtesy he could show.

As they watched him, smiling, the Children of God disappeared the same way they had appeared, with flashes of light.

"All the Children of God have declared the Glorious Assembly to be over. This meeting will hereby be adjourned. May the blessings of the Great God Roux be upon all of you who attended this Glorious Assembly."

And so, the Glorious Assembly came to a close.

It was the beginning of the end.

CHAPTER
SIXTY-SEVEN

Cough.

Shea looked down at the blood on her palm and let out an exasperated laugh. *Goodness. Me, coughing up blood twice in such a short span of time? You think you've seen everything, and yet—*

"Shea!"

"Lady Shea!"

"Don't move!"

"Your wounds!"

She heard everyone freaking out as she chuckled to herself, but she paid them no mind. It wasn't as if she was going to die. She wasn't meant to die yet.

This was a punishment.

Petty payback from my father, who was very displeased by my actions. He's such a jerk.

Cough.

She clucked her tongue before she coughed up even more blood. At times like this, it was nice that her body wasn't able to die, but that didn't mean it didn't hurt. And it hurt a lot. She wondered if she'd ever felt so much pain.

Maybe it feels worse because I barely ever use my powers.

Regret surged through her, just a little. "Why did I make that damn promise, anyway?"

How did this even happen? she wondered as her vision went blurry.

"Shea, no!"

"You can't fall asleep! Shea! Shea!"

Shea slowly closed her eyes to the sound of loud voices calling out to her, as a lullaby. It occurred to her that she might be going to sleep for a while.

Upon returning from the Glorious Assembly, Edward and the others were greeted by utter chaos.

"Your Imperial Majesty! The destruction of the southern guardian stone has been confirmed. As soon as the power was gone, trees and vegetation shot up from the ground, leaving the land unfit for cultivation. Many of the commoners' houses have ended up on top of the trees and are no longer habitable. The whole South is in a panic because so much of the land has been taken over by trees."

"With the destruction of the southern guardian stone, the last of the wards has disappeared, and we're receiving countless reports of strange phenomena all over the empire."

"Some of the soil has been reclaimed in the West, but the soil is in no state to be cultivated. It's similar to the barren soil in other nations during a drought. Crops will not be able to grow there this year."

"The tsunamis in the East have subsided, but the trade ships were wrecked and the saltwater from the tsunamis has saturated the soil, killing the crops."

"The cold front has dissipated in the North, but the crops have frozen. They're asking for urgent aid."

They had never seen such a level of chaos. Along with the unending stream of messages and reports coming in, documents flew through the air.

Eid felt conflicted as his officials handled this chaos with poise, each of them staying on top of matters, making reports, and not being confused by outdated documents. He wondered whether he should be proud of them or pity them.

Ace's mouth dropped open in awe at this magical sight.

The most exasperating thing was that they had just returned from a meeting that had concluded that nothing could be done about any of this.

Unsure of where to begin tackling this mess, Ace stood deep in thought, and Eid wondered why they shouldn't give up. It was meaningless. The empire had never been worth much to Eid to begin with.

The same went for Edward, but he wasn't someone who could stand by and watch things happen.

"Sir Edward, we've dispatched the knights, but they're saying they can't do anything about the rampant pillaging of the nobles' food storehouses."

"Let's go," Edward said.

It was his loss, as he also wished to have a future with Shea. Eid watched Edward in silence. He respected him, but that was it. He turned and walked away, ignoring the voices urgently calling out to him.

"Your Imperial Majesty! Where are you going?"

"Sire! Sire!"

Watching Eid leave, Ace had a feeling.

"Lady Sistina." Unless she came back to life, not a single person alive would be able to move him now.

The emperor of Vencroft was a special being. Though he didn't have the power to bring someone back from the dead, he was blessed by the Great God Roux. By ascending the throne, he kept the empire from falling to ruin. This was why there had never been anyone else on the throne than someone from the Vencroft bloodline, even though there had been countless revolts in the empire since its foundation.

But now, there was only one remaining member of the Vencroft family. Only the emperor—who had no interest in keeping the empire afloat.

Ace had practically been brainwashed into acknowledging that his duty as a Maxwell was to make sure the empire didn't fall to ruin. He couldn't give up here, even though the thought occurred that the empire had gone on long enough.

His weak excuse was that he felt bad for those who had sacrificed themselves. In all honesty, Ace wanted to live a little longer. He didn't want Vencroft, this empire, to fall during his generation.

"Shea Grande."

And so, Ace made the decision that he knew he must not make.

"What is the emperor doing?"

"The fields and houses are gone. We can't even fathom what to do next year, let alone this year!"

"We have no idea what to do to earn a living next year."

"My house, give me back my house! It's your duty to protect this empire."

"We paid our taxes, so give us what we're owed."

It wasn't only the imperial palace that was in chaos. The situation in the capital was far worse. People who'd lost everything to the sudden change in environment crowded around the palace gates and the town center, screaming and yelling at the top of their lungs.

The market was the same. Food prices had hit an all-time high.

"Give it to me. Hand it over!"

"You have to pay for it."

"I did!"

"Like hell you did! It's one gold coin, not one silver coin, you thief. I'm going to alert the guards."

The citizens had no way to afford the constantly rising food prices. Thanks to the ongoing blessing and the reasonable rule of the emperor, the poverty level had never gone over 0.3 percent, earning Vencroft the title "the miraculous empire." To its citizens, who had enjoyed the empire's blessings for hundreds of years, the sudden inability to afford food was outrageous and unacceptable.

It was perhaps only natural that things led to extortion and violence. Humans tend to lose their minds when faced with unreasonable circumstances. This led to nothing but chaos.

Chaos drenched in blood.

A man looked down at this chaos, partially amused, partially empathetic, and partially empty. "Amazing how they act exactly according to my expectations."

Noise may not have lived thousands of years as Griffith, but he'd lived freely among humans for hundreds of years, as his title "of Freedom" suggested. He smiled a bitter smile at this expected chaos. Though things had never been this bad, the guardian stones of Vencroft had weakened in the past, creating chaos and selfishness in the affected regions.

Like now. Humans couldn't let it go. They'd become entitled to what was merely a favor. They weren't mature enough to let go of that entitlement. They had countless excuses, and it always ended the same way.

He was sick of it. "How do they never change?"

Shea, also watching the chaos through her spyglass, smiled coldly, and answered Noise's thought as if she could hear him from afar. "Because they are foolish—foolish, arrogant, and selfish. It's hard to overcome your own nature."

Because, as always, human nature was idle and averse to change. Because humans couldn't let go of their wealth, of everything they owned. And so, they revolted, as if they couldn't change.

Not all humans were like this, but the few of them who were more prone to such behavior influenced the rest, who jumped at the chance to act out what was already latent inside of them. A few humans weren't like this, but they were too few to go against the majority, and they would end up sacrificing themselves and leaving this world.

No matter what era, this was always true.

"There is always a price to pay for the luxuries you have enjoyed. But it's too late now, no matter what sacrifices you make. The time you earned by sacrificing Eid Roux Vencroft was limited. You didn't think it would last forever, did you? Did you really?"

Ace looked up at Shea with an expression he'd never shown anyone else.

"..."

"Ace Maxwell. I suppose I ought to welcome you, since you came to my café."

"Shea."

She gave him a joyful smile. "Welcome to Sangria, Mr. Hypocrite."

"The Maxwells must assist the throne and put the safety of the empire above all else."

Ace had grown up hearing this lecture from his father.

It wasn't only him. Abe and even their cousins had to listen to this mantra repeatedly as they grew up. It was a tradition in the Maxwell household. The Maxwells lived their lives according to this motto.

Though Ace hated this at times, he didn't always hate it. Since being a Maxwell meant working in the imperial palace as the right-hand man of the emperor himself, at the very center of authority, it wasn't all bad. There were many members of the imperial family, but Ace only interacted with Eid. They grew up together.

CHAPTER SIXTY-EIGHT

Just because Ace was close to a certain prince didn't mean the Maxwells were protecting him, nor did they plan to. The Maxwell family was loyal to the whole imperial family. It was unwritten law, so Ace's closeness to one of the princes wasn't a problem. They were the same age, so it was only natural.

And more importantly, Eid was a prince who had nothing. All he had was his bloodline. He'd been excluded from the fierce and bloody fight for the throne and had no intention of becoming the emperor. Even if he had, it would have been hard with no one supporting him. Eid was positioned to receive a title and a small fortune so he could leave the imperial palace and live in peace, just as he wanted.

"If someone hadn't meddled with the fate."

"..."

"Right?" Shea smiled bewitchingly.

He smirked in response to his own reaction. Rather than bewitching him, her smile made him feel uneasy. "How much do you know?"

"Is that what you want to know?"

"No. Of course you'd know everything. You're a superior miracle worker and the great Shea Grande, after all."

He was sure there was nothing she didn't know. The miracle workers were aware of everything that occurred, although they never raised a finger. But even without those abilities, this was Shea, the woman who was bound to know everything about the imperial palace's—no, his—blunders.

"And I'm a friend of Sistina Illid Vencroft," she added, "a friend of the woman whose blood of sacrifice you justified with your petty hypocrisy."

"She made the decision herself."

"Oh, my. I didn't know you were capable of saying such garbage." Shea added that she'd assumed he was another boring man.

Ace gritted his teeth at her obvious insults. He was overcome by fury, even though he knew he had no right to it. He prayed she wouldn't notice.

Shea was far too quick. She smirked as she noticed the fury in his eyes. "Hypocrites always end up like this. They speak of justice but end up acting unjustly and are left angry as they cling to their hypocrisy. They're all the same." She was almost impressed by this sameness.

Ace gritted his teeth again, feeling as though she was referring not only to himself but all the Maxwells before him.

"Please, that's enough. You know very well that nothing good will come if you provoke me."

It was a pathetic attempt at a threat. Naturally, it was complete nonsense that didn't affect her one bit.

"It'll at least improve my mood, and I have nothing to lose from it. Don't you know you're undeniably inferior to me?"

"…"

"This generation's Maxwell, with his back against the wall, perhaps the last of his kind."

Though he knew very well that he didn't deserve to even look at her face, Ace felt the urge to punch that bright smile off her face.

Why did I have to be a Maxwell? The thing he'd lamented a hundred times since that day came back to him.

The Maxwells, who pretended to be more righteous than anyone else, were merely pretenders. The necessity to maintain a façade of righteousness and virtue, only to engage in various dirty deeds and betrayals, was devastating to the mind. If he hadn't been born a Maxwell and chosen as the successor, he wouldn't have had to endure any of this.

In fact, his twin brother had no idea about their family's true nature. Abe was living according to the righteousness everyone expected of the family. Ace was the greedy one, and he'd almost automatically taken on the role of successor. But at times like this, he resented Abe.

It must be nice... not having to do any of this. No, you would say you couldn't do it... because you're a righteous and virtuous Maxwell... even though I'm the real Maxwell.

"How much do you—never mind. That's a dumb question. Do you want me to beg?" Ace bent down to get on his knees. It was something he should've done already, but the thought of getting on his knees filled him with shame. He had never gotten on his knees, even in front of the emperor, the actual victim of his crimes.

Most people would dissuade someone from kneeling, but Shea looked as though she couldn't understand what he was doing. "What use are your knees to me? It's not like this will bring Sina back."

"..."

She scoffed, as if what he was offering was nowhere near enough. "The only way for you to get rid of that spineless guilt of yours is for Sistina to come back to life. That will never happen, so don't even think of being rid of your guilt. Just live with it."

"Shea."

"Why are you looking at me like that? You knew this would happen, and yet you made the choice yourself."

"...!"

His eyes widened further than they ever had. His gaze wavered, almost trembling. No one could've known what she'd said.

"Kill her. Don't let anyone find out."

Because none of the people who knew about it were still alive. He'd made sure of that.

"No secrets last forever, right?" Her smile confirmed it.

"Shea!" Ace was unable to keep his cool. He raised his voice.

"Ugh, you're too loud," she complained. "There's no need to shout. Did you think you'd get away with it, like some common thug?"

"That's not what I—"

"It's why you came to see me. You want me to help you out—because I have the power. You'll do anything. As if you'd sacrifice yourself, when all you did was take someone else's life so lightly, like the other Maxwells before you."

"…!"

"The Vencroft family continues to be victimized by your family's petty sense of justice. The citizens are your next victims, and now me."

The Maxwells were the closest allies of the Vencrofts. They were there every step of the way, by the side of every Vencroft, until their deaths. But on the flip side, the

Maxwells were twisted and cruel. They should have realized that what they were doing was wrong, after all they'd done.

If they'd been human beings.

Shea's gaze turned cold. She hated the Maxwells. She hated their arrogance and the way they sacrificed countless lives in the name of honor, claiming that it wasn't for their own good but for the good of all, always convinced that they were on the side of justice. They were worse than garbage.

She couldn't think of any reason to go easy on Ace, especially because this measly guilt of his came from an injured sense of pride at the idea of committing some unspeakable sin. He was a Maxwell through and through.

And that's why he was the successor.

"Just as we revealed during the Glorious Assembly, we're not going to do anything about it," she said. "All this is the result of the Maxwells' sins, which have piled up. You should have let it end when Aslan said. Why did you sacrifice us to keep Vencroft tied down, only to pay a much higher price now?"

"How did you—"

"How could I not know the history of my own kind? You must have thought you were justified. You must have foreseen that a Vencroft without the Vencroft blessing would descend into pure chaos. But did you really think there would be no consequences for choosing one of us as a sacrifice to destroy the Vencrofts? Did you think the curse of the imperial line would be the end of it, even though you used it to your advantage?"

"...!"

Thud.

Ace collapsed, falling to the floor as if he could no longer face the horrible truth.

Emperor Aslan. Known to the public as another troublesome emperor, his was a name the Maxwells could never forget. He was the greatest victim, a reminder of dark deeds they must never forget. Emperor Aslan was the start of the Vencroft curse. The man who forcefully claimed a Child of God for himself and was cursed for it. The man recorded in history as having committed a grave mistake because of his lust.

But history is recorded by the victorious, and the truth couldn't have been any more different.

"Aslan was a good emperor, wasn't he?"

You were the ones that made him go insane. Ace squeezed his eyes shut at her declaration, which sounded like a death sentence. His mind went blank—because she was right.

Aslan Roux Vencroft. His reign had been a golden age for the empire, and he had been a wonderful ruler. He was skilled, selfless. He valued peace, which led him to avoid conflict with other nations. He set up the abundant farmland of the West, raising the quality of life for his citizens.

And none of this was recorded in history. The Maxwells had seen to it.

Emperor Aslan had predicted that the Vencroft blessing would eventually run out and fade away completely. He'd also predicted that the longer the blessing lasted, the more the people would feel entitled to it and eventually become too dependent on it. So, he made sure that the empire would thrive even without the blessing. He wanted the Vencroft blessing to end with him. It became quite weak.

But the Maxwells refused to let it fade. They broke him and caused him to take on the curse, thereby strengthening the blessing.

The curse affected all the Vencrofts, but it didn't affect them equally. Depending on their individual character and capabilities, it was possible to overcome it.

But none of them did, because the Maxwells made sure they couldn't.

"Because by letting them go insane as a result of the curse, the blessing would be strengthened."

"It's a secret the Maxwells must forever keep hidden, especially from the imperial family."

"It was inevitable. Otherwise, the blessing would—"

"So, what if it faded? Nothing will go wrong from the blessing disappearing. You're well aware of this. You sacrificed the imperial family because you wanted an easier, more abundant life. Are you saying those who were sacrificed for such a trivial matter would understand? Can you bring yourself to tell Eid?"

"..."

"You, who killed Sistina in the end in order to make Eid go insane, to complete the curse?"

Ace was rendered speechless.

He wanted to say something, but his mind went completely blank.

CHAPTER
SIXTY-NINE

"Nothing comes free in life, and you should've known that anything gained through someone else's sacrifice has its limits. We will do nothing, and that won't change no matter what you do."

"..."

"It's time for you to save the day yourself, don't you think?"

There was nothing he could say.

Being a villain took a lot of energy. The same was true for being good, but being purposefully malicious toward someone was truly exhausting.

"Playing the villain doesn't suit me." Shea turned away from the dazed Ace and went up the stairs and flopped onto the bed, lamenting how tired she was.

She didn't want to care about any of this. It had been forced upon her, and it exposed her to an endless stream of exhausting circumstances.

It wasn't like she'd asked for much.

"Why did you have to choose something like that?" *It was one of your many possibilities—one of your many fates. Why did you have to choose this when you had so many choices? Unlike me, who has no set destiny.*

She couldn't help feeling resentful, meaningless as it was. The person she wanted to question was already dead.

Creak.

"Shea."

I guess I'm not in a position to complain.

"I thought it would take much longer for you to get away from work."

She had no idea when Edward had entered the house. She gave him a slightly sad smile, and he carefully opened the door and stepped inside.

She was conflicted. She wanted him to visit but also hoped he wouldn't. Because of the covenant she'd made, there was nothing she could tell him, and she knew this would create a rift between them. But if he stayed away, that would be painful too. In the end, she'd always made decisions for him, for his own good. *That probably wouldn't have sat well with me.*

"Come in."

But you always come back to me, as if you don't have any other option. And that makes me happy. I can't help myself.

He was the only one who made her feel human, even though she had far surpassed humanity.

"You're not going to tell me, are you?"

Of course not. Shea faintly smiled. Even if it hadn't been for the covenant, she'd never intended to tell him. It would only hurt him. "Sometimes ignorance is bliss, Ed."

And there are some things that I don't want you to ever know. You probably have some of those, too.

Unable to think of anything to say, Shea smiled.

Edward couldn't help but relent, as he always did. "I know you're not telling me for my own sake."

"..."

"Otherwise, there'd be no reason for you to keep it secret from me. You can't even be bothered to lie—because you hate complicated things."

Shea flinched. *Wow, look at this guy. Did he get his memory back, or something? How did he get it so fast?* She couldn't help feeling attacked. She really did hate trying to make a lie sound plausible, which only led to more lies. She preferred to shoot down an opponent with the bitter truth.

Edward watched her react before stepping close and wrapping his arms around her in a tight embrace. He nuzzled his face against her shoulder. "I know you, so please remember this."

"And what might that be, darling?" She responded to his sweet gesture by raising her arms and hugging him back. She had every intention of listening to whatever he had to say.

"That I would do anything for you."

"...!"

It could be taken as clichéd sweet talk, and she knew they were just words, but she couldn't help freezing in place, even though she knew he would notice.

He tightened his embrace and continued, as if to get a promise out of her. "So, Shea, promise to tell me when the time comes."

Because I will do anything.

As if he were trying to extract a promise from her, even if she didn't reply—or perhaps he was promising it to himself... as he squeezed so tightly that it was hard for her to breathe. All she could do was hug him back, gazing at her lover who never changed. It was almost heartbreaking.

"You've already done so much," she whispered. She knew that he meant it. He'd already done so much for her.

It was more than enough.

After the Glorious Assembly, Eid locked himself in his room and refused to do any work, despite the chaotic state of the empire.

Crash! Riiip!

The members of staff at the palace waited with bated breath at the violent sounds coming from his room every day. He ordered that no one disturb him, and the officers who came to see him backed off at the sounds they heard. No one dared to open the door. They knew that it could very well be their lives getting shattered and ripped to pieces, like the objects he was destroying.

Having successfully secluded himself inside the imperial palace, Eid was in his right mind. He tilted his wine glass, his expression eerily composed. After confirming the truth at the Glorious Assembly, the gift that Shea had given him—the gift of amnesia—faded away. And as it did, his memory returned like raindrops seeping back into his mind.

Eid accepted the truth. He didn't want to miss any moment of it. Overcome by emotion, he destroyed quite a few objects, but even that made him feel ecstatic. Every moment he'd shared with her could only be joyous memories to him. Even the most mundane moments had been blissful. All his happiness had been concentrated in that short period of his life.

And so, when he returned to reality, he went through a cycle of deep depression and the loss of motivation.

Only when his emotions had settled down did he remember something.

Elias, the boy.

The child he'd met just once in Sangria, the cheeky boy who had called him good-looking. It was strange that he couldn't forget the boy, despite having met him only once.

"Shea must have gone through a lot."

When he looked back on the memory of meeting the boy, he realized that he looked exactly like Sina. He could understand now why Shea had been so disgusted when Eid had first shown up at the café.

After watching you go, how worried must she have been that the child who looks like you would suffer the same fate?

Even the boy's cheekiness reminded him of Sina. It was a devastating thing to tell a parent.

That cheekiness was what brought you to me, but as a parent, it must be exasperating to watch. How did you not realize how anxious I was that someone else might be as lucky as me? I was always so on guard. You really...

"...never understood how much I love you."

He would've been ecstatic to hear that she was pregnant. She would've told him the news with that lovely, flushed face that he loved beyond anything in the world. He'd never wanted a child, but if she'd told him he was going to have one, he would've been happy, without a doubt. Because it was a child with her. She was his truth and his meaning in life. His previous values meant nothing.

So why didn't you tell me? If you did, then…

"I wanted you to be alive, rather than the boy."

…maybe I wouldn't have felt like this.

The fact that there was a living, breathing link between him and Sina made Eid overwhelmingly ecstatic. But still, he wanted her more than he wanted a child.

If you were still here, nothing else would matter.

"Sistina, why didn't you take me with you?"

I should've died instead of you. It would've been better for the boy. For everyone. Because I'm nothing but an empty husk without you.

He rubbed his face and let out a weak chuckle.

Oh, maybe this is why you never told me. Neither you nor Ace.

Ace Maxwell typically told him to stop spewing nonsense when he brought up a successor, or a wife, but he hadn't said a word.

Ah, so you knew. I suppose it's inevitable. You are a Maxwell, after all—and a Maxwell assigned to me. Of course you knew.

Ace must have kept quiet for the sake of the empire.

Or perhaps part of it was for me.

The Maxwells existed to make decisions for the good of the empire. But this was Ace, imperfect, kindhearted Ace. When Eid regained his memory of Sistina, he also remembered Ace awkwardly dragging around behind her—the great Ace Maxwell, completely at the mercy of a woman.

It meant that Ace had liked Sistina.

But Eid had no intention of resenting Ace for letting her die. No one could stop a Vencroft gone mad. Not only was he the emperor, but as the recipient of the Vencroft blessing, no one could touch him. Only someone permitted by Roux could do so, or someone working through some other means.

Something like poison, for example.

"...!"

Another memory rushed back.

"But—"

"You must feign ignorance. I am still the head of this house."

"But you don't have to kill her!"

"Yes, I do. Only then will the curse be complete, and the emperor will be unable to stop it."

"But it isn't her fault!"

"It isn't. Who would have thought she was a blessed being? We must get rid of her before she cancels out the Vencroft curse

completely. Only then will the curse be complete. We bear no ill will against her."

"Father!"

"You're still too soft. We must get it done before Marquess Zestia finds out. I will take care of this, so all you must do is pretend not to know anything."

"How am I supposed to... Father, father!"

"It can't be."

The weight of the returning memory caused Eid to drop his wine glass.

Crash!

As it shattered on the floor into a million pieces, a shard cut Eid across the cheek, but he didn't even notice the pain.

What in the world is this memory?

CHAPTER
SEVENTY

This can't be.

Eid reeled, disoriented by this strange memory, as yet another memory flooded back.

"Run away!"

He staggered, his vision blurry. He instinctively sensed the oncoming danger and struggled to hold onto his senses, but she didn't listen. She never listened.

"Eid, Eid! Come back to me! Don't let it win!"

"Sina... You can't... hurry."

"This can't be happening. No, you can't give in now, Eid."

Sina had suddenly coughed up blood.

Through his blurry vision, he could see he was holding a knife. A knife covered in blood.

Even as her eyes widened in shock, she managed to smile.

Her smile had been...

"Si...na..."

...heartbreaking. As if she'd known this would happen.

"…!"

He was sure of it, even though it had happened so suddenly. And then there was the "blessing" he'd heard in the other memory.

His mind reeled in chaos.

Whenever he was with her, he felt strangely calm, and the bouts of fury that sometimes overtook him completely stopped. All that was left was a man who could be happy.

But if that was thanks to the blessing, why did the curse suddenly activate?

"Do not fool yourself. You will not be any different!"

"…!"

Why?

At that moment, Eid recalled the words his father had yelled before his death. Perhaps those words weren't desperate nonsense, after all, but words of experience.

"Haron!"

"Yes, sire! You called for me?"

"Where is Ace—no, where is Duke Maxwell?"

"Duke Maxwell? I heard that he was on a trip abroad until he heard what was going on in the empire and is now hurrying back, but…" Haron, the head of the palace staff, looked flustered at Eid's urgency, but he remained calm, a testament to how long he had served the emperor.

"When did you last hear from him?"

"Three days ago."

Eid solemnly drew a hand over his face at Haron's reply. "Damn it. Haron, prepare my uniform—no, fetch me my shoes."

Though it was very unprofessional, Haron floundered at the sight of Eid reaching for his sword even as he gave the command. "Pardon? Do you intend to leave the palace?"

"Yes."

Haron fctched the emperor's shoes at top speed. Eid quickly put them on and hurried along.

There was no time. If he was right...

"Where are you heading, sire?"

...then Shea was in danger.

"To Sangria."

"Father?"

After his crushing defeat at Shea's hands, Ace had been cooped up in the palace, doing nothing but work all day. When he returned home that night, he rubbed his eyes in disbelief at the sight of a familiar figure. It was his father, who'd left to enjoy a late honeymoon with his wife and left

Ace with his duties. He hadn't even replied to Ace's pleas to come home when the first guardian stone was destroyed.

No matter how much Ace rubbed his eyes, nothing changed. He felt like bursting into tears when he finally realized his reliable father was really here.

"What took you so long? And where is mother—"

The manor was strangely quiet. If his mother had returned, the manor would have been full of life. His mother was like a warm spring breeze, and her presence warmed any place she happened to be.

"Father?"

And more than that, his father was acting very cold. It was a demeanor he never had in front of his wife. He was like the quintessential noble, harsh and cold.

Ace had seen him act like this only once before: the day of *that* incident.

Ace felt like he had been drenched in ice-cold water. "Why are you here, father?"

Duke Maxwell eyed the wariness and distrust in his son's eyes and clucked his tongue. "You are still too soft. I thought you might've changed a little, since you have experienced it now."

"Father, that's not what I'm referring to," Ace said sharply, unwilling to back down. "What are you up to? What unforgivable sins are you planning to commit this time?"

He, too, was a Maxwell, and he'd agreed to do what had to be done. But he wasn't coldhearted enough to do such things without being affected by them. Once was enough. He couldn't handle doing something so atrocious a second time. His father was right. In the end, he wasn't able to put aside his conscience. He was nothing but a foolish hypocrite, having gained nothing and unable to let go.

But that didn't mean that he was willing to give up on his humanity. He could no longer give up on anything. Not anymore.

Only then did Ace realize why Shea had been so harsh toward him.

Oh, now I understand why you said those things. Like you said, it might be better not to have any powers at all—if they were going to bring you to the brink like this.

"You have to turn a blind eye once more."

"How am I supposed to do that?" Duke Maxwell seemed to be completely ignorant of his son's thoughts and feelings.

Ace despaired at the chilling command. Again. He was going to do it again. Simply standing by was agonizing. He wondered whether his father knew how horrible it was to watch and do nothing, whether he knew what he was ordering him to do. He feared he couldn't handle any more of this.

The duke wordlessly retrieved a small bottle from a safe, even as he watched his son despair.

"You really don't care about your own son, do you?" Ace said.

"You may be my son, but Vencroft has tens of thousands of citizens."

Ace let out a weak laugh at the way his father seemed to recite a line from a script. Shea had been right about everything. The Maxwells were horrifying hypocrites. He felt so disgusted with himself that he didn't think he would ever be able to face her again. "Did you ever regret it, father? Aren't you racked with guilt?"

His father strode past him without any hesitation whatsoever. "It's been a long time since I've forgotten it. Stop remembering. It will only eat away at you." He resumed walking away, as if he had no intention of letting Ace raise any objections.

Ace shed a tear as he listened to his father's footsteps echo down the hall. "You are a true Maxwell, father."

I'm sorry. I'm so sorry. In the end, I wasn't able to do anything.

"Forgive me, Sina."

Weak chuckles echoed through the quiet mansion. He sounded like he was about to burst into tears.

Jingle.

Edward and Shea were enjoying afternoon tea at Sangria, which was as peaceful as always, when the quiet afternoon was broken by a wave of knights crowding into the café around someone else.

"Wow, I knew the Maxwells weren't in their right minds, but I never thought it would be this bad." It wasn't every day that Shea was genuinely impressed. Her comment was so uncharacteristically genuine that even Edward, who'd kept his guard up, felt his nerves relax.

Fortunately, this applied to their opponents as well. Edward placed his hand on the hilt of his sword as he scanned the group of knights that had barged in. Each and every one of them were well-trained fighters, at least above average. With nearly twenty of them to deal with, even someone of Edward's skill couldn't help but be on edge. There was a huge difference between fighting alone and having to protect someone while you fought.

The leader of the knights made his way past the wall of knights to stand before them. Edward's fingertips twitched ever so slightly as he recognized the man, but he tried not to show it.

He hadn't quite believed it when Shea said the name Maxwell. In Edward's memory, the man had always been a model noble, a man who always put the good of the empire first, who loved his family and looked out for the less fortunate.

Duke Maxwell, who seemed not to notice what was going through Edward's head, faced them with the coldest expression Edward had ever seen. "How could those with great responsibility be on the same level as common folk?"

"You've always been great at spewing nonsense." Shea had no interest in indulging him.

Duke Maxwell let out an exasperated laugh. "Yes. To you, it may seem like nonsense. Our continuous demand for sacrifice cannot sound reasonable to you."

"What you're saying sounds like nothing but mockery to me, when you're never the ones being sacrificed yourselves. And yet, you hypocrites believe that dirtying your own hands constitutes sacrificing yourselves. What is it that you want? My dear hypocrite?"

"I hear that my son has bothered you."

"Oh? Compared to you, your son is a complete angel. How could you even compare him to a true Maxwell? I wasn't bothered." She smiled brightly, clearly implying that it was him and his knights who were a bother.

Having spent many years in politics, Duke Maxwell clearly understood the meaning behind her words. He didn't let it show and ignored her biting comment. "My son still has a lot to learn."

"A father who teaches his son something he need not know—what a great father. So, what is the reason for your visit?"

"Oh, nothing much." He shrugged, not letting her mockery bother him. He was so nonchalant that even Edward wasn't able to react in time before he brandished a knife. "I'm only here to do what I must do as a Maxwell."

As underhanded as I expected. "Well, you seem like a true Maxwell indeed."

Everyone drew their swords and pointed them at each other.

The timing was perfect.

CHAPTER
SEVENTY-ONE

Everyone froze breathlessly in place, trembling with unbearable tension.

Shea looked far too calm for the circumstances. "Is this the Maxwell solution? To get rid of me?"

"Of course not. We couldn't possibly treat a Child of God like that."

"It might be better than whatever you're planning. You really are terrible. So do you intend to make me your puppet?"

"That would be nice—if it were possible. The powers of the Children of God can only be used by their own free will, and I know that even you have restrictions when you use your powers. I'm not that stupid."

Shea was genuinely impressed at how he didn't hesitate to speak his mind. "Oh, my. You know quite a lot about us, even more than the imperial family, it seems—maybe because you're the ones in control. I suppose that means you have some use for me other than my powers. That doesn't sound very pleasant."

"I would be grateful if you cooperated."

"Then I'd like to ask you for a favor, too. Would you kindly piss off? My eyesight is too precious to be ruined by the sight of you."

I may not have asked for any of it, but I grew up smothered in love and attention, you know.

With that, swords began to clash. The sound of sharp metal making contact rang throughout the café.

Edward's skill as a sword master didn't go to waste, as he took on several knights on his own.

"...!"

But even he couldn't stop all of them at once. The knights he faced were also experienced swordfighters, though they hadn't yet earned the title of sword master. Their advantage was in their numbers; thus, they attacked him simultaneously.

Two of them got past Edward to charge Shea. Edward tried to leap toward her, but he wasn't able to shake off the knights, who were working together with great determination.

"Shea!"

Shea remained calm even as he desperately called out to her. Nobody could comprehend how she remained so calm. She opened her mouth, her expression as nonchalant as ever. "Fel."

"...!"

As soon as she spoke, every blade pointed in her direction shattered into pieces. Everyone gasped at this astonishing sight.

Fel appeared in between them. "I thought you'd never call me."

"Didn't you want me to?"

"Perhaps."

Nobody dared to comment on how indifferent the two of them sounded. His obvious mastery justified his unperturbed demeanor.

"So, it *is* you, Fel, the former knight captain," Duke Maxwell said. "I see now that I should've brought many more knights—and I would have—if I'd known there would be two sword masters. Don't you think this is unfair?"

"You were going to overwhelm us with numbers, and now you're complaining about fairness? Do you have any sort of conscience?" Shea's voice dropped to a mumble. "Oh right, that's the first thing you got rid of."

Someone else appeared from the crowd to agree with Shea. "You're right, I'd like to know that as well."

"Eid?"

"Your Imperial Majesty?"

Everyone turned to look at the emperor in shock.

Shea, again the only one remaining calm, let out a low groan. "Wow, and now the fool makes an appearance. It must be a special day today, Fel."

"I suppose so," Fel agreed. "An especially terrible day."

Shea gave him a round of silent applause, then turned to Duke Maxwell with a smirk. "Now that the greatest victim of the Maxwells has appeared, how does the proud head of the Maxwells feel? Full of regret, perhaps? Or frustrated?" She would have bet gold on the latter.

Duke Maxwell gritted his teeth at her obvious sarcasm.

The situation couldn't be worse for him. The one person who could never find out about any of this was the emperor. This was an emergency. If Shea opened her mouth and revealed the secret, the curse would grow stronger, weakening the blessing at the same time. Without anyone else to take the throne and the Vencroft blessing, it would be disastrous for Eid to fall to pieces.

"Hyle Maxwell, there was something you should have told me first before taking things into your own hands like this." Eid's expression was one of clear fury.

Duke Maxwell remained surprisingly calm.

I suppose he's the emperor for a reason. Shea took the opportunity to scan Eid with her abilities, searching for the blessing she had granted him. Though it was unstable, it was still in place. That meant that he hadn't fully remembered everything. Then again, if he had, he wouldn't still be on his feet.

As strong as Eid was, it was as easy to crack him mentally. And yet, he acted as though he had remembered everything. She couldn't help being impressed. He must have so much practice putting on a brazen face.

Duke Maxwell, unaware of any of this, gritted his teeth. The worst-case scenario was playing out before him. However, he didn't feel any regret. He'd been living as a Maxwell for decades, and as befitting of a true Maxwell, he firmly believed that this was for the good of Vencroft. "Everything I did was for the sake of the Vencrofts."

"Everything you did was due to greed." Eid's smirk was deadly.

"Of course you would think that. One day you will realize the truth, Your Imperial Majesty."

"…"

"Because you are the emperor of Vencroft."

"You're consistent with your bullshit." A culprit who not only insisted on having done nothing wrong but also tried to make the victim understand his logic was without a doubt the worst kind of person. Eid made this very clear by the way he glared at Duke Maxwell.

The culprit himself was too absorbed in his own delusions to notice. "You don't need to understand. You need to keep being the emperor."

"That makes me want to step down at this very moment," Eid replied with a huff of laughter. He was being sincere.

"You'll never step down, sire."

Duke Maxwell was convinced that no one could relinquish the privilege and power that came with the highest position in the empire. He believed all humans were the same, including the emperor. There may have been past emperors who genuinely wanted to step down, but they hadn't, not only because of their inability to let go of greed but also because they had things to protect by remaining emperor. Duke Maxwell was certain that Eid was no different.

Unfortunately, there was something he didn't know.

"I can step down at any time," Eid said.

"Sire, that is ridicul—"

"I only took on this role because I didn't want to die at their hands. And after that—well, you were the one who destroyed the one person I wanted to protect, weren't you?"

"...!"

The one person I wanted to keep safe.

Duke Maxwell bit his lip when he realized the truth that Eid made plain for him, his face devoid of any expression. He had forgotten. He'd gotten rid of the one person that Eid Roux Vencroft wanted in life, for the sake of the empire. He'd gotten rid of her without a second thought, because the curse would take away Eid's memory and he would continue to sit on the throne with no desire to move.

Duke Maxwell had ignored his son, who begged him to change his mind, and gone through with it.

Eid eyed Duke Maxwell before giving his last command as emperor. "Capture Duke Maxwell."

As soon as Eid uttered this command, imperial knights surrounded them.

"Be careful," he added. "Those knights are highly skilled."

"Yes, sire!" The imperial knights began to arrest the other knights.

Shea wondered why the duke and his knights had even bothered showing up. "Hmm? Wait—it's over already? Nothing even happened."

"Is that not preferable? There's less to clean up," Fel commented wryly as he put away his sword.

Shea looked around. "There may not be much to clean, but we have a lot to replace."

"..."

Some of the tables and chairs were completely broken. Fel fell silent as he glanced at the craters and cracks across the floor and walls, the result of the release of the sword master's aura.

Shea paid him no mind. "I guess we can have the imperial palace reimburse us. Or maybe the Maxwell family."

"...!"

"Shea!" Duke Maxwell, making his way past the imperial knights, charged toward her. It happened so suddenly that the knights couldn't restrain him. He pulled his arm back and threw something directly at her.

Everyone cried out to her in a panic, expecting a cursed item or some sort of explosive.

But Shea remained calm, once again.

Shing!

The object was cut in half right before her eyes. Fel wouldn't allow whatever it was to reach her.

"...?"

It was just a medicine bottle.

Who throws something like that? There were no poisons or acids in this world that could burn someone on contact. This medicine wouldn't have any effect unless she drank it.

They stepped out of the way a split second too late. Fel barely got splashed, but Shea was drenched.

"Hey!" Shea cried, her hair now plastered to her face from the mysterious liquid.

"I apologize," Fel immediately replied.

Getting hit in the head was never fun, but the fact that her whole head was drenched, liquid dripping down her face, made it worse. Shea's mood was completely ruined.

CHAPTER
SEVENTY-TWO

Shea resisted her flaring temper and began to wipe her face with her hands. "What in the world is this, anyway? His smug face makes it worse."

"Let's dry you off," Fel said. "Please don't use your hands."

Recaptured by the knights, Duke Maxwell looked immensely pleased with himself. He didn't attempt to resist.

Fel, feeling that something was off, handed her a towel and warned her not to use her hands to wipe off the liquid.

Disgusted at Duke Maxwell's smile, she grimaced as Fel handed her a towel. She wondered what in the world this liquid could be that made Duke Maxwell look so confident. She carefully sniffed at the wet towel.

"Come on!"

"Shea, please!"

"Shea!"

Outraged cries erupted all over the café at her reckless behavior, but she didn't pay any attention to them. She continued to sniff the towel before looking up in exasperation. "It's just water."

"What?"

Shea let out a baffled snort. "There is a bit of a pleasant smell, but it really is water. It seems like it's from a mountain spring."

"Are you sure you smelled it properly?"

"Of course—I'm a cook, you know. My sense of smell is excellent. Go ahead and smell it for yourself."

She handed over the wet towel to make sure, a bit outraged at having her senses put in question.

Fel trusted Shea but couldn't help feeling suspicious about Duke Maxwell's confidence. He carefully raised the towel to his nose and looked up, mirroring Shea's expression. "It does appear to be water. Holy water, perhaps?"

"Right?" *I told you so!*

Ignoring Shea's huffy outburst, everyone turned back to Duke Maxwell. It made no sense to throw this at Shea so desperately.

Duke Maxwell remained composed, seeming certain that something was about to happen.

Even though nothing had happened so far, everyone grew nervous at his unwavering confidence, and they looked back at Shea.

She raised her voice. "I'm totally fine. He must've made some sort of mistake. Maybe he got scammed."

"Only a fool would believe everything they're told," she added, even in the face of evidence to the contrary. The others began to think that she was right.

Duke Maxwell's confidence waned as well, seeing that no one appeared concerned and Shea seemed unaffected. "That... That's impossible!"

He finally dropped his façade. His true face, the one that had been hidden behind his mask for decades, combined all the selfishness and egotism in the world.

How disgusting, Shea thought.

"The holy water of the first holy grail has always had an effect," the duke continued, "even on the Children of God."

"Ah, so that's how you cornered Sistina." Shea's lips spread into an ominous smile. She finally understood the situation, thanks to Duke Maxwell's outraged outburst. "You know, I gave her every kind of blessing I could, because I was worried about her working at the imperial palace. It was easy—because she was already beloved by Roux. I made sure she was as blessed as she could be, so that nothing could hurt her even at the vile palace, but..."

"..."

"...when she died, I realized those blessings had been tarnished."

"...!"

She burst out laughing, as if she were enjoying herself. But the dangerous glint in her eyes made it clear to everyone that she wasn't amused. Her gaze became so cold that no one dared to speak up.

There was one man who couldn't ignore what she'd said. He clutched her arm, his gaze wavering wildly.

"You blessed her?"

Shea wondered what she should do as she looked at Eid.

"..."

"So, she could've just stayed by my side?" His voice trembled with despair, and the fingers clutching her sleeves were desperate.

Nothing good would come from him knowing the full truth. And Sistina had asked her for that favor because of this. He knew this as well, and yet he was asking for an answer. She pitied him, but at the same time, it annoyed her. He might be pitiful, but at least he was still alive. Her stupid friend, the friend she hadn't wanted to lose, hadn't even gotten to stay alive.

Though her friend wouldn't have wanted this, Shea decided to be a little mean for her sake. "It was a blessing from the seventh Child of God, the Child of Life. I'm much stronger and closer to perfection than the other miracle workers, and I don't give out blessings left and right."

Blessings tended to get weaker the more they were distributed. The Children of God rarely ever blessed anyone, but the blessings they did give were incomparable. Shea's blessing of Life was strong enough to deflect anything that would put the person's life in danger—if Shea wanted to protect them.

"When Sina told me that she chose you, I tried to change her mind, but in the end I failed," she said. "But I didn't want her to come to harm, so I blessed her as much as I could."

"So?"

"Normally, it would have been impossible for her to be killed in any way, even at the imperial palace, as long as her blessing was intact. Unless someone tampered with that blessing."

She was supposed to have stayed alive. Shea had made sure of that. Her blessing had been tarnished; fate had chosen death for her friend.

"Holy water from the first holy grail, huh?" she continued. "That would be the first holy grail ever, bestowed by the Goddess of Fate, and the holy water made by the first Child of God. Holy water with this much power should be able to affect most God-given abilities, including my blessings."

"..."

"So Sistina stood no chance." Eid's arm fell to his side. His expression was empty, as if he had no more energy to think or even stand.

Shea moved past him to stand in front of Duke Maxwell. "But you seem to be misunderstanding something. This only affects normal abilities—those with a little bit of power. It won't do anything to any of the nine Children of God. It certainly wouldn't hurt us. Did you think holy water would negatively affect the Children of God?"

"…!"

"A regular user of divine power might be overwhelmed by the incredible difference in power and become physically exhausted or have their fate twisted, which might make them temporarily more susceptible to attacks. This might affect them if they're unlucky. But if they adjusted to the holy water, it might even strengthen their powers. We Children of God have maxed-out stats, so of course it wouldn't affect us."

"That's impossible! So far, it has always—"

"If it did work, it was bad luck on their part. I don't quite understand why the Maxwell family has this, but I'm guessing this is it. So, it's over, right?"

"Shea Grande," the duke growled.

"How wonderful," she replied lightly. "Seeing you make a face like that has been on my bucket list for a while.

Goodbye—oh, and I never want to see you again, so watch yourself."

The way he looked up at her was pathetic. She couldn't stop smiling. Feeling generous, she waved her hands at the knights in a shooing motion. They dragged the duke away.

The itch she had felt for years was finally scratched, leaving her satisfied. She was turning around to have Eid pay for the damages when chaos erupted behind her.

"Your Imperial Majesty!"

"Eid!"

"Isn't Eid Roux Vencroft the end of the Vencroft bloodline?"

"Don't say that!"

"We must take him to the palace."

Shea frowned in confusion. Her café had turned into some sort of emergency room, with people shouting and voicing their worries and anxiety. She let out a huff of exasperation as soon as she caught sight of Eid, whom she'd left behind a moment ago. The blessing she'd given him had nearly evaporated, and the curse of oblivion was rapidly taking hold.

"Wow, he looks like he's about to die." She shook her head, tutting and mumbling about how weak he was, to everyone else's indignation.

"Shouldn't you do something?"

"Well, it's his fate," she said with a shrug. "And he brought it upon himself, so..."

Shea felt a bit bad. A small part of this—actually, a lot of it—was her fault. But she didn't want to get involved. She tried to ignore what was going on.

"Viscountess. Viscountess!"

It took a moment for her to realize that one of the knights was calling out to her.

CHAPTER SEVENTY-THREE

"If anything happens to His Imperial Majesty right now, the empire will fall."

"Help us, please."

Shea frowned at the knights. "That's not really—I mean, not that I care."

"Please, Viscountess!"

Do they teach them how to beg at the knight order or something? These guys are relentless! The way they begged at her feet, refusing to let her go even as she tried to kick them off, was too much. Shea shuddered with disgust. "Ugh, fine. Just let go, will you?"

"Really? Will you help?"

"You little... Let go of me this instant."

"Yes, ma'am!"

She kicked a few of the slower knights out of the way and stepped closer to Eid. He lay as still as a corpse. With the curse of oblivion developing so rapidly, he must have been in a lot of pain. The memory of going on a rampage to kill Sina must be returning and being erased in a constant loop.

And yet, he looked surprisingly peaceful. The way he seemed at peace with the idea of dying right here, right now, rubbed Shea the wrong way. He couldn't die yet. For the sake of that foolish girl who died in his stead so he could live, Shea couldn't sit by and watch him die in peace.

Over my dead body.

"Get out of the way."

"Shea." Edward faced her nervously. Though he was worried about Eid, he didn't want Shea to use her powers and get involved. He wanted to tell her not to do anything, but he couldn't watch his friend fall into the abyss.

Shea seemed to know what he was thinking—because she avoided looking at him. "All of you, stand back. It could be dangerous if you get swept up."

Even as she gestured for everyone to back away, she worried a little. There were restrictions on who she could save, due to the oath she'd taken, but she had a feeling this would work. Eid Roux Vencroft had already paid the price, and he was the only Vencroft, at least in name, left in the empire. He couldn't die like this. Not yet.

She decided to try.

"…!"

"This is—"

When she held her hand over Eid, golden light flooded from it. Her lips formed into a relieved smile as the golden light twinkled.

Thank goodness. If Eid had died like this, I wouldn't have been able to look you in the eye when I see you again in the afterlife. "All right. Done!"

"That's it?"

She used her ability so rarely that she could count the times on one hand, and it had been so long since the last time that she barely remembered it. "He should wake up soon. I haven't used my powers in a while. I'm tired."

The others seemed a bit confused at how fast it was over, having expected something more grandiose from a Child of God. They glanced between Shea and Eid in a daze.

Shea ignored them and stretched her arms, exhausted.

Eid blearily opened his eyes.

Everyone was properly impressed and awed by Shea's divine powers now that Eid had awakened so quickly. The Children of God were truly powerful.

"Can you hear us, Your Imperial Majesty?"

"Eid."

Shea ignored the stares as she took Eid by the chin and turned his face this way and that. "Hmm, he might be a bit out of it for a short while. His eyes are not focused."

The others were so distracted by Shea that no one was able to stop what Eid did next. He lashed out and scratched her across the arm. "Don't touch me!"

"…!"

Shea was as surprised as everyone else. It was such a deep scratch that she was bleeding. "Ugh, what a warm thank-you for someone who saved your life."

Blood dripped down her arm. She would have loved to pay him back double, but her temper faded when she saw Eid mumbling to himself, clearly unstable.

It was only those around her who fretted, as usual. They dispersed to find something to stop the bleeding, disinfect the wound, and dress it. Utter chaos, once again.

"It'll stop in a second," she said, "so stop running around."

"What if it doesn't?"

"It's not a deadly wound, and we Children of God can't die whenever we want to. Stop worrying."

"Shea!" Edward sounded genuinely upset at her careless attitude.

Even as she covered her ears at his outburst, Shea felt no sense of dread. She knew everything. She wasn't the one they should be worried about, because she wasn't fated to die at this point.

You should be worried about yourself.

But she couldn't tell him. She knew he wouldn't care what happened to him, even if she told him the truth, because he was kind and foolish.

Which explained why he was angry at her right now.

"You don't need to worry, you know—" She suddenly felt sick.

"Shea?"

This wasn't something like nausea. Shea knew this feeling.

Cough.

"Shea!"

She had coughed up blood—again.

Everyone scrambled to her side.

Shea tuned out their footsteps. *Wow, I can't believe I've coughed up blood twice in such a short span of time. Life is full of surprises.*

She let out a huff of laughter at the palm of her hand, covered in her own blood. The holy water that Duke Maxwell had thrown at her—now she could see why he'd been under the impression that it would do something to her.

I see. It was you, father.

There was no other explanation. The reason holy water affected those with divine powers was because it put a stop to fate, which blocked *his* direct influence.

Because the worst catastrophe to befall us Children of God has always been the god himself, their father.

She couldn't help but laugh.

"Lady Shea, please don't move."

"Your wound."

Despite her father's attempts to influence things and bring her to his side sooner, Shea sensed that he wasn't able to change her fate that much. Shea wasn't meant to die yet. Fate wasn't going to let her die here, even if her father wanted it, and he knew this too.

So, this was another punishment. Petty revenge from her father, who seemed very displeased with what she'd done.

You are insanely petty.

Just as she clucked her tongue, Shea coughed up more blood.

Cough.

It was nice that her body couldn't die from something like this, but it still hurt. She wondered if she'd ever been in so much pain. It was probably worse because she'd used her powers.

Damn it. This is why it's better not to have any powers. I don't remember anything good ever coming from having these powers.

"Why did I have to go and make that promise?"

Why did things turn out like this? She felt her consciousness fading away.

"Shea, no!"

"You mustn't fall asleep. Shea, Shea!"

The desperate voices sounded like the voice she'd heard that one day, a long, long time ago. *I won't die this time, but will I end up traumatizing you like that again? I'd rather not.* Knowing that she might be asleep for a while this time, Shea hoped he wouldn't cry too much before she closed her eyes.

Just like she had that day.

"Shea!" A desperate voice echoed throughout Sangria.

Edward shook her as he grimaced in utter despair, but Shea's eyes refused to open. He clutched her tighter. He felt as if the ground was falling away beneath his feet, plunging him into the abyss.

Everyone began to panic as they tried to think of the best course of action.

"Get ahold of yourself, please."

"Call a physician."

"No, we should move them both to the palace."

Fel stood rooted to the spot. He slowly squeezed his eyes shut as regret took a firm grasp of his heart. *Should I have gone down to the country when you told me to? Maybe I should've left when you first told me I could leave at any time. I should've let the bottle hit me instead of cutting it in half.*

If Shea had been awake, she would've told him to get a grip. Fel found himself chuckling weakly as he imagined how she would react. But what could he do?

You're the one who did this to me. You're the only one I have left now.

Though he could see her lover falling apart, Fel thought that the emptiness he felt was far greater. Unlike Edward, who was a duke and had countless friends and things to protect, Fel only had Shea.

What am I supposed to live for without you?

He thought himself weak and pathetic. A sword master, although he thought his title "hero of the empire" didn't suit him. He had nothing to live for if the person who'd held out her hand and told him to lean on her when he had nothing left were to disappear.

He gritted his teeth to keep himself grounded. She wasn't dead yet. And she had assured him that she wouldn't die so easily.

 SEVENTY-FOUR

Fel wanted someone to reassure him that Shea wasn't dead and that they could help her. He wished for it desperately.

And his wish came true.

"Look at you. It's like a funeral in here."

"…!"

Everyone's eyes widened in surprise at the man who put his hand on Fel's shoulder.

Fel was the only one not surprised. He was ready to get on his knees to thank the man who had appeared like a miraculous answer to his wishes. "Sir Noise!"

Noise grinned and said, "Yo."

"I wasn't quite convinced when you suddenly appeared and said we had somewhere to go, but you were right. This is a sight to behold."

"Right? I knew I had a weird feeling."

"I never thought I'd ever see Lariana in this state."

Noise hadn't come alone. He brought aides, as if he'd known he might need more people.

"Ruperto of Memory." Edward looked up at Ruperto even as he clutched Shea closer, as though his world was falling apart. This was someone he'd seen at the Glorious Assembly.

Ruperto smiled softly in recognition at Edward's voice. "You were one of the men at the Glorious Assembly. You must be Lariana's lover? The great man who conquered her heart."

"…"

Edward looked down at Shea. She was fast asleep and didn't look like there was any life left in her. His heart sank. But he couldn't leave her on the cold floor.

Ruperto spoke again. "Sir, would you carry Lariana to her bed?"

Regaining some of his senses, Edward picked up Shea and headed toward her bedroom. His silence suggested he still wasn't in the right state of mind, but it could have been much worse.

Noise and Ruperto exchanged glances, letting out sighs of relief.

Fel took charge of the knights and said, "The rest of you, take His Imperial Majesty and go back to the palace."

"Yes, sir." The knights moved to tend to Eid.

Fel hurried after Edward and arrived in Shea's bedroom, where Noise and Ruperto were checking on her.

"Hmm, there doesn't seem to be too much wrong with her."

"She *is* the Child of Life. Her body is healing quickly."

"The problem is that her father seems to be bothering her."

"He's practically bullying her," Ruperto said. "If this goes on, she may end up stuck in sleep for years."

Noise tutted his tongue in disgust.

Ruperto's frown agreed. "He seems to be forcing her soul to sleep."

"That probably means she's in the past right now. You could get stuck there forever, couldn't you?"

"But this is Lariana. She'll return eventually. She went there because of his interference, so she'll be able to return. Her fate won't allow for her to be stuck there."

Edward spoke up. "Does that mean she can't wake up?"

His voice was so full of worry that the two men took a moment to consider how they should answer.

"She'll wake up eventually if we leave her be. But we don't know how long it will take."

It wasn't much of an answer.

"Anyone could say that! Please, I'll do anything, so—"

"We're here to check on her." The two men looked conflicted at his despair.

Edward realized that there must be a way to bring her back, judging by their expressions. He clung to them in desperation. "Please tell me what I can do. I'll do anything. I'll even put my life on the line—if it's necessary."

Ruperto shot a glance at Noise, clearly wanting Noise to make the decision.

Noise was faced with a dilemma. Edward was not going to back down, so he gave in. "You're the one who'll have to deal with her wrath, all right? You have to keep her from trying to kill me."

"Of course!" Edward had no confidence in his ability to stop Shea from doing anything, but desperation made his answer instant.

Ruperto raised his eyebrows at Noise and raised a mumbled complaint. "I don't want to die yet."

"Me, neither."

"You're a grandpa ready to return to dust, but I'm still a young man, you know."

"Hey! Our age is meaningless, and I still look like I did when I was in my late teens!"

"But you're old enough to be a great-grandfather."

Edward, having no patience left for this, finally put himself between them to end their frivolous argument. "Please tell me what to do."

The sword master, who could no longer control his own emotions, began to emit an aura of pure malice. As superior as they were to humans, the two Children of God, weren't immune.

"All right, fine. Please stop being so scary. I'm starting to shake."

"We're vulnerable to auras, so please stop. Lariana is the only one strong enough to not be affected by things like this."

"You're used to her, so you may think she's the standard, but she's a total beast compared to us. We're fragile, you know."

A Child of God with God-given powers, fragile? It sounded like complete nonsense, but the two men looked deadly serious as they awkwardly scratched at their arms. They were revealing sensitive information about the Children of God that could be used against them, but the two sword masters in the room cared more about Shea than the empire.

"I'll pay any price necessary, so please..." Edward spoke with firm will. He seemed ready to give up his life.

At the mention of paying the price, the two men immediately turned around.

"The Shea you see here is basically an empty shell. To put it simply, she has no soul. Her soul is on a journey against her will." Noise mumbled something else about "that nasty old man's fault." His bright smile couldn't hide his fury as he concluded his simplified explanation. "All journeys come to an end, and so will hers. The problem lies in how long it will take. The way to get her back faster is to go and get her yourself."

"Myself?"

"Yes. You must go into her mind, find her, and bring her back."

Edward realized why the two men had initially hesitated to tell him this method. Going into someone's mind didn't seem like an easy thing to do.

"There's the distinct possibility that you will become lost in her mind, and more importantly..."

"You'll see all Shea's past and memories."

"So?" Edward didn't understand why that might be an issue.

The other sword master, on the other hand, understood why this was a problem.

The two men looked at Edward in disbelief and outrage.

"Did he say 'so'?"

"He did. Unbelievable."

"She must've acted so innocent around him."

As expected of Shea, even her acting skills were extraordinary. The two men seemed genuinely impressed by her, although they didn't say much else. They didn't want to die. But they thought this might work.

"As soon as Shea finds out that we saw her memories—oh, man."

"But this is her boyfriend. She's not going to kill him."

Probably. Noise swallowed the last part, but everyone in the room understood what he meant. They were clever enough to understand the implied meaning behind his vague explanations.

"I am able to send you into Shea's mind with my powers. However, please be warned."

"..."

"My powers are able to place you inside Shea's mind, but they cannot protect your own mind."

Going into someone else's mind was incredibly dangerous. Even with the help of divine powers, the risk remained. There was no way to protect the invader's mind from being influenced by the things he might see.

Edward felt surprisingly calm, even as this risk was explained to him. It was as if he didn't recognize this risk as being dangerous. Shea was most important to him, and his own safety didn't even register as a priority.

Ruperto felt like he understood, as he looked into Edward's steadfast, almost frighteningly twisted eyes. He understood why Shea had chosen this man, why she hadn't been able to tell him anything. There was no way, especially since she knew what he was capable of. Ruperto could tell what this kind of man would do if he were to find out the truth. He wouldn't be able to accept it. Even they themselves, the Children of God, couldn't accept the truth and had given up instead.

Ruperto had a lot to say, but he didn't say any of it, because Edward was about to see everything.

"I have only two things to tell you. First, the past is simply that—the past. You won't be able to change anything easily, and I urge you not to even try. It wouldn't put you in danger, but it could completely mess up Shea's life and lead to never seeing her again. No matter what you witness, let it happen."

"I understand."

CHAPTER
SEVENTY-FIVE

Ruperto almost laughed at how quickly and without hesitation Edward answered. It was easy enough for Edward to say that he understood, but Ruperto knew it wouldn't be that easy. None of the Children of God were very open about their pasts, and Shea had been the most secretive.

"Lastly, you cannot return until you find Shea. If she says she doesn't want to come with you and refuses to return, you can still come back, but not with your own abilities alone. You'll have to risk your life."

"Couldn't have asked for anything better," Edward seemed almost happy with this warning.

Ruperto stared at Edward in astonishment and shook his head. He wondered how in the world she'd come across this man and took a moment of silence for the hardship she must've gone through because of him.

"I'm the one who'll die at Shea's hands," he finished. "So, please be careful."

"I will."

"Then let's begin. Please take Shea by the hand and lie down next to her."

As he activated his powers, Ruperto hoped for one thing: *"Let this damn power—the power that I never wished for, like Shea..."*

"Now, close your eyes and think of Shea."

...not be the one that hurts you.

"May blessings be with you."

"Hayeon!"

"Ugh, what?"

"Class is over, you know."

"Oh, is it time for lunch already? Thanks."

As soon as he entered Shea's mind, Edward was faced with a girl who wasn't Shea. She was wearing clothing he'd never seen before in an environment entirely unfamiliar to him. She seemed quite young.

"Someone drag me to the cafeteria, please. I'm too sleepy to walk straight."

It was a young girl who looked nothing like Shea.

"How in the world does this girl get better grades than I do?"

"Because I'm smarter than you?"

"Ha. Do you want me to leave you behind?"

"My bad."

But for some reason, Edward could tell immediately that this girl was, in fact, Shea. It was strange.

"You can't live like this, Miss Hayeon."

"Life isn't that great, though. Can't I cruise along?"

"I totally agree with you, but you can't."

"How long are you two going to keep going?"

"I'm starting to get bored, so we'll stop here."

"I'm getting hungry."

The small crowd of girls walked down the hallway together.

Edward followed the girl as if he were in a trance. Her life was simple. She studied, ate, then came home to an empty house and went to bed. Her home had a completely foreign, seemingly illogical layout in his eyes, but what made it even less like a home was that no one else was in it. She was entirely alone when she fell asleep, and even after she woke up again and got ready to leave, no one else was in the house. It was like she didn't have a family.

"Hayeon Chae."

"Yikes!"

"At least you finally noticed me. You practically had your eyes closed when you came in."

"It's late enough to come in with my eyes closed." But she did have a family. "Wait, dad's here, too? Is something going on today?"

"We have something to discuss with you." She actually had both parents. "Are you going to bring your lovers here so we can meet?"

"Then that includes you, too."

"Ugh. Just give me your money. I don't want the rest. Just leave me a nice, chunky inheritance."

"That might be an issue."

"Right?"

They acted more like her friends than her parents. There was very little affection between them, almost as if they were only associating with each other because they were related by blood or on paper. They weren't at odds with each other, but the important parts of being a family were missing.

"Then I'm going to bed."

"Hold on."

"It's midnight. Time for all the good boys and girls to go to—"

"Hand over your report card before you go."

Edward wasn't the affectionate type, but because the Griffith family was one of the few noble families with sincere caring and love for each other, he could tell exactly what was missing here.

"Oh? Since when did you care about my grades?"

"I need them to show off."

"Oh. Fine."

Though they were family, they weren't really family. They were more like a group of people thrown together out of necessity. But the girl Hayeon didn't seem to mind. Perhaps she was used to it because this was how she grew up, or perhaps it was her personality. He had a feeling it was both, but in any case, he was relieved. It wasn't ideal, but he didn't want her to get hurt.

It was the same way he felt about Shea. He held back the hand that prepared to reach out to the girl as he realized one thing for certain. This was Shea's past life. This was Shea before she became Shea Grande.

But it was strange. Just because he'd entered Shea's mind didn't mean he should be able to see her past life. Humans didn't remember their past lives.

Shea had been hiding something.

"Hayeon finally lost it."

"She's all loopy."

"You try getting up at six in the morning and being forced to help your mom pick out an outfit."

"Oh God."

Shea Grande was a reborn person.

Edward committed Hayeon's life to memory without getting bored even once. The life of a high schooler was incredibly repetitive, but that didn't bother Edward. He couldn't help feeling enthusiastic about the fact that he was finding out things about Shea he hadn't known before. He listened closely to the most mundane conversations and never tore his gaze away from her, even though he was supposed to be looking for the current Shea, not the Shea of the past.

He forgot about his objective as he watched Hayeon. The more he watched her, the more familiar she seemed, even though he'd certainly never seen her face before.

"Wait, did you reject another one?"

"Another what?"

"The guy who asked you out earlier."

"Who?"

"Ugh!"

It could be because she was essentially Shea, but there was something more to it. It was as if he'd known her.

"You're not supposed to ask Hayeon things like that."

"Yeah, she barely even remembers a straightforward profession of love. Do you really think she'd remember an implicit one like that?"

"That's true."

"When are you going to get a boyfriend?"

For some reason, Edward felt like he knew what she was about to say. Not because he knew her so well, but because it felt like he'd heard what she said in the past. Like he still remembered it. He felt like she'd said something like *"I'm not sure if I'll ever bother."*

"I'm not sure if I'll ever bother."

Edward's eyes widened, even though he'd been certain she would say those words.

"You sound like someone who's already been through a hundred boyfriends."

"If someone manages to get past my laziness, I'm sure I'll end up dating them."

"Is that even possible?"

"I'll bet money on it being impossible."

"We're talking about you, you know?"

Edward's expression froze in confusion. The conversation seemed so familiar, even though it made no sense.

"Curse this subject—*Bwah!*"

The scene suddenly changed, and Hayeon tripped while carrying a heavy stack of notebooks.

"Watch out!"

Someone jumped in lightning quick and cushioned her fall, so that she wouldn't hit the ground.

"Ow."

"Are you hurt?" Even though he was the one to hit the ground hard, cushioning her fall perfectly, he was entirely focused on Hayeon's well-being, as if he didn't care about himself.

Hayeon seemed so surprised and confused by the boy's laser focus on her that she stuttered. "Oh, uh, nuh-uh. But shouldn't I ask you that?"

"I'm glad you're safe." The boy beamed, pleased by the fact that she was safe, completely ignoring her question whether he was okay.

Hayeon stared at him in awe. She couldn't take her eyes off him.

The boy had achieved something countless boys before him could only ever dream of: He'd made an impression on Hayeon.

After that, Hayeon kept staring at the boy as if she were in a trance.

"Hayeon. Hayeon!"

"Hmm. Hmm?"

"What's up? You keep zoning out. Did you see a ghost or something?"

Even her friends noticed, but she didn't seem to be able to control herself. Her gaze was drawn to him.

Hayeon realized a few things then. First, the reason her gaze was drawn to him was because he was always staring at her.

"Stop looking at her, Gwonhyeok."

"Yeah, Hayeon is out of everyone's reach."

"Not only is she a goddess, but it's like she's a wall nobody can even hope to climb."

"Exactly. Don't even get your hopes up. She made a lot of guys cry for staring at her, you know."

Second, even his friends knew how interested he was in Hayeon. He had a reputation for having no interest in any of the other girls, because he was so busy looking at her.

"Do you know that guy? Gwonhyeok?"

"Duh. All the girls know him."

"Every girl has talked about him at least once."

"I mean, look at his face. He's ridiculously handsome but he doesn't utilize it, and some of the girls he's rejected go around badmouthing him for it."

"But calling him an orphan is definitely crossing the line."

"Do they really need to do that because he rejected them?"

"I get that they felt hurt because he never even looked at them—but yeah, it's too much."

So Hayeon did something very unlike herself, without her friends' knowledge.

Thunk.

"Hayeon?"

"I don't like owing anyone anything, so tell me what you want."

"What I want? I don't need money or anyth—"

"I never said anything about money. Who are you, my lackey? Why would I give you—wait, did you get hurt enough to go to the hospital? Then of course I'll pay for your medical bills."

CHAPTER
SEVENTY-SIX

It was very unlike her to bring up something about someone before they had the chance to speak.

"N-no, I didn't get hurt."

"You're not lying, are you?"

"I'm not!"

"All right. I'll believe you."

"But I'm not lying."

She smiled because she thought he looked pretty when he was flustered. "Sure, sure. Now, tell me what you want. I have to repay you somehow."

"Well... food, maybe?"

"Oh, nice. On weekdays, I only have time in the evenings. Is that okay?"

"Same for me. We're both students."

"That's true. All right, then how about dinner tonight?"

"Sure."

After this, they gradually began to spend more time together. Gwonhyeok began to talk to her first as well.

"Hmm?" Hayeon said. "I guess I dozed off. Let's go home."

"I like you."

"Hmm?"

"I like you, Hayeon."

Hayeon gave him the brightest smile he'd ever seen. "I almost died waiting to hear that."

The two of them became a couple, and they had everything they ever wanted in each other. They seemed happy. They didn't seem to lack anything. They were perfect, and no one at school dared to come between them.

As Edward watched them, he sensed the truth.

This boy was him.

Noise pulled the covers over the two lovers sleeping peacefully side by side.

Ruperto grimaced, as if he found him despicable.

"Are you happy now that everything went the way you wanted?"

Nobody in the room seemed surprised that everything was unfolding according to someone's plan. Both the man who had remained silent throughout and the man who was acting as planned had known this from the start. The only one in the dark was the fool, so fixated on Shea that he saw nothing else. He had played right into someone's hands. It was almost pitiful, yet no one spoke a word, for Edward's sake.

But it still didn't feel good.

Ruperto glared over at the root of all this, his eyes narrowed in displeasure.

The root of all this gave him a satisfied smile. "Yup. I feel so much better now."

"You can take the blame later."

"Hey, now. You helped, too."

"The mastermind is supposed to take the blame."

"Wow, how mean." Noise pouted.

Ruperto glared at him again, exasperated at the man's incredible audacity.

With at least some sort of conscience left, Noise avoided his glare and cautiously voiced his sincere opinion. "I was being kind, in my own way." *You probably wouldn't have wanted any of this, though.* He chuckled to himself as he imagined Shea's reaction. "She may act like that, but Shea is a total softie."

Shea probably wouldn't agree, but Noise sincerely believed this. Just as she didn't entirely hate father, even though she despised him so much.

"I wonder if you would've thought of this trick." *You probably never asked for our help in case it might bring us harm.* "I hope you like the birthday present I prepared for you."

"…"

"Happy birthday, Shea."

You would probably demand a more normal present instead—since you're so foolishly kind.

His friends shuddered at the statement he didn't even need to voice, but Gwonhyeok didn't care. He looked happy and whole. No one could say otherwise.

"Hey, man, I know you're crazy about Hayeon, but…"

"Yeah. I think you're crazy at this point."

"It's fine," Gwonhyeok replied. *Because I have Hayeon.*

His friends had all kinds of things to criticize him for, but when they saw how happy he was, they couldn't bring themselves to say anything. He lived for her.

"Hayeon!"

"Yikes! Wait, when did you get here?"

He didn't need anything else as long as he had the girl, who didn't hesitate to accept his embrace. "What's wrong with your face, Gwonhyeok?"

"Well…"

"You pulled another all-nighter, didn't you?"

He would do anything to make this happiness persist.

Edward couldn't stop watching his former self, reading the clear emotions on the boy's face. As he continued to watch, Edward began to remember. He really had been like this in the past. He'd been an orphan with no money, no background, and no family, but he hadn't felt like he was missing anything because he had so much to live for.

"That's not what I want from you. Please take care of yourself."

"..."

"You're not the only one in love here. Try to remember that, okay?"

Because he had her. He had Hayeon, who loved him with all her heart, even though she thought it was too embarrassing to tell him "I love you."

Those days had been full of joy. And just as happiness had found him so suddenly...

Shink!

"*Ahahahaha!* You should've chosen me instead!"

"...!"

...it left him just as suddenly.

"Do you know how much I loved you? How dare you betray me like this!"

Stab. Stab.

"Why did it have to be Gwonhyeok? Why not me?"

Did he really want to know the answer? Even as he watched the scene again, he couldn't help but curse. How could anyone do this to her?

Edward was filled with rage, but that rage left his body as soon as he heard the part he hadn't known before—her true feelings.

Even as she wavered in the face of repeated stabs...

"Ah, my poor guy is going to cry..."

...Gwonhyeok's Hayeon had only thought of him, even in her moment of death.

Edward hadn't known this. Tears spilled down his cheeks. He couldn't help but rejoice in the fact that she'd worried about him, even as she was dying.

I don't deserve you.

The scene changed. The environment was the same, but the sunlight looked different. He realized right away that this was something that happened after Hayeon died, something she couldn't have known. He couldn't tell whether it was because he was here or because she somehow knew about what had happened after she had died.

But what followed was the past he remembered.

"Hayeon?"

"You there, boy! Don't go any closer."

"Oh God. Dude! Hold him back!"

"We're so sorry! He's her boyfriend."

The place was covered in so much blood that it was hard to believe it had come from one person. The pretty girl who'd turned so many heads was nowhere to be seen. To him, she was still the prettiest girl in the world, but he'd never imagined he would see her face covered in blood, the tear trails evident among the bloodstains.

"*Ha! Haha…*" He laughed weakly, even though this was nothing to laugh about. He could feel everyone looking at him as though he had gone crazy, but he didn't care. The tears flowed as he laughed. The taste of those bitter tears… it was the worst thing he'd ever tasted.

"Get a grip, dude."

"Yeah, you're still alive. You need to stay sane."

He couldn't understand what his friends were saying. *Why? Why do I have to live—when the person I lived for is over there?*

Now that he thought about it, this was probably their awkward way of trying to console him, but the words didn't reach him. He'd already lost his mind.

"Let go! Let me go!"

Her mother ran toward him. She had always tried so hard to look beautiful, and yet she was a total mess, missing a slipper. Pushing aside the policeman, she rushed over and grabbed him by his collar. "It's your fault, it's all because of you! If she hadn't met you, my daughter wouldn't have died."

"Darling! Calm down. You know it's not this boy's fault."

"Why not? He's just as guilty! You heard what that bastard of a murderer who killed my daughter said!"

The psychotic murderer's confession had been enough to drive her mother insane: *Because she didn't love me.* No parent would be able to bear such an insanely nonsensical reason.

He didn't resist as she hit him. He welcomed it, in fact. He wanted someone to punish him—because she was right. He was guilty.

That day, he lost his reason to live.

In the end, the murderer was set free. He didn't even go to jail. He was too mentally unstable, despite his confession and the clear evidence that he'd killed her. His father was a powerful man, so the murderer ended up at a mental facility instead, more of a luxury hotel than a mental facility.

Her parents, who had sincerely loved her though they hadn't known how to show it, slowly went insane and ended up getting a divorce. He was exasperated at all the things they realized now that she was dead.

Everything in the world was laughable, and nothing seemed to elicit emotions from him anymore.

Why did you leave me behind in a world like this?

"Why? Why? Why did you leave me? Why did you leave me behind? You should've taken me with you. Why did you go alone?"

He resented her, just a little. She should have taken him with her. He knew she never would've done so even if she'd had the ability, but he still wished for it.

And in the end, he fulfilled his own wish, the moment he pierced his own heart with the knife he used to kill the man who had murdered her.

CHAPTER
SEVENTY-SEVEN

"How foolish and pitiful of you, my child. You weren't meant to die this way."

He didn't care. He had no reason to keep living.

"Do you really believe that?" somebody asked him.

He didn't know who it was, but he answered the voice anyway, stating that no life was worth living without her.

The person replied to him. "If you want to see her again, you'll have to pay a big price. You may take on more than you can bear."

His eyes shot open at the idea that he could meet her again. The voice seemed worried, but he couldn't understand why. Any price was worth paying, if only he could see her again. He didn't care how miserable his life would be otherwise.

As long as he could meet her again.

"My simple and lovely child, it will be very difficult. *He* is very jealous, you see, and he will not allow your presence."

He? Who might that be?

The voice, which sounded female, chuckled at his confusion, and bid him good luck. "I hope you do your best until the very end. I would like both you and that girl to find happiness."

And when he opened his eyes again, he'd been reborn as Edward van Griffith. He had lost his memory of his past life, but she was etched into his very soul. He could never forget her.

In the end, he found her again, and they reunited.

Beautiful dark blue hair fluttered in the breeze.

As he watched all this happen again, he wondered.

If you knew all this, as you watched me stare in awe into your golden eyes...

"Ha. Unbelievable."

...what thoughts ran through your head?

Shea Grande's new life was perfect.

"Come here, my darling, my beautiful sweetheart!" her mother called.

"Mm?"

"Mommy's home! I made a lot of money."

"Perfect" wasn't enough to describe it.

"Present!" Shea cried.

"You cheeky little girl. Your dad is getting it right now."

The Grande family was the embodiment of joy, as if to make up for her past life.

"Please get me smaller presents."

"Small presents aren't my type."

Shea grimaced. *Mom, you're supposed to follow the recipient's tastes, not your own.*

The mother laughed brightly at her daughter's exasperation, and the father smiled pleasantly at the sound of their laughter. The household staff chuckled as they watched the family.

It was perfect. They lacked nothing.

They did have *some* problems.

"Mom! Did you cook again?" Shea exclaimed.

"Why do you look at me like that whenever I cook?"

Shea huffed at her mother's audacity and responded immediately, sounding totally exasperated. "Because the results are always a mess."

A mysterious mass bubbled up from the pot, as if she'd cast some sort of spell and made the ingredients come alive. Shea staggered back, unable to bear the sight of whatever horrible liquid was inside the pot. She looked scared that it would lunge out and consume her mother where she stood.

But both Edward and her mother knew that she was terrified of the person who created the monstrosity before her.

"Darling, would you please refrain from backing away from something someone put their heart and soul into?"

"I'll stop if you throw that out outside right now." *Wait... maybe that would be bad for the soil.*

Her mother pouted at her daughter's sincere aversion. She furrowed her eyebrows and went back to cooking, determined to show her daughter something impressive.

Shea felt genuine fear as she watched her mother. "Dad, dad! *Daaad!*"

Her father heard the urgency in her voice. Since she was extremely mature for her age, her calling out to him like this was rare.

But he found himself at a loss for words upon seeing the brutal sight that greeted him. "Darling! Why are you cooking?"

"It's been a while since I cooked for you, so I wanted to."

Her father pulled out his hidden ace. "It *has* been a while—so we should go out to eat together."

"We can do that anytime. We should cook at home when we're here."

"Th-then leave it to me. You're going to hurt yourself."

He made more attempts to get his wife to stop, but all of them failed.

Dreading the increasingly likely future in which they would have to taste her mother's horrifying creation, Shea opted for the last resort. "Mom!"

As her mother turned, she somehow managed to tilt the pot, which fell over and landed on the ground. "Hmm? Yikes!"

Everyone was startled because it had happened so quickly, but thankfully no one was hurt.

"Please be careful," Shea said.

"Sweetheart, you're scaring me. Please don't look at me like that."

"Yeah, right. You're banned from the kitchen from now on, mom. dad..."

"Oh, right. Yes. Shea seems to be very upset. Darling, let's get you out of here to check if you got hurt anywhere." He dragged her out of the kitchen.

Shea sighed and started cooking. She seemed very experienced in the kitchen.

As he watched her, Edward was certain that Shea remembered everything from her past life.

"Ugh, my back."

As mature as children could be, it was unusual to sense the soul of someone older in a small child. And Edward had seen exactly what happened. Shea disguised it as an accident, but she definitely used her divine powers to knock over the pot. Her parents seemed to be unaware of her powers. It seemed that Shea had been freely using her divine powers since she was born. And she probably knew that she was a chosen Child of God. Shea, the woman he loved, was very intelligent and quick on the uptake.

"Mom, dad, let's eat!"

"Ooh, as expected of our wonderful daughter. You're the best."

"Yup, I am—so stop coming to the kitchen, mom." But the fact that she pretended nothing was wrong and lived as their daughter, getting better at cooking with each passing day, meant that she loved them.

Besides the fact that she was chosen, Shea had a delightful life. She had a beautiful face that suited her eyes, which were the color of molten gold, and her dark blue hair, which had changed color when she awakened to her God-given powers. The family wasn't rich, but they were perfectly comfortable, as well as wonderfully bright and humorous.

"Shea! Shea!"

"You're going to trip, Sistina."

"No, I w—*Bwah!*"

"I was going to say, I'll eat my hat if you don't trip."

"I don't know what that means, but it's mean."

Shea also had a precious friend. Her friend's hair was wavy and poofy, resembling cotton candy, and she had golden eyes that shone brighter than Shea's. She was the embodiment of brightness.

Edward thought of his unfortunate friend as he watched this girl. *Oh, so this is the girl you loved.* He could see why Eid had fallen for her. Even if she hadn't been Shea's friend, she was full of charm.

"Were you practicing with your sword again?"

"This is the best way to defend yourself against humans that don't deserve mercy. And it's a good workout. Do you want to join me?"

"My brother will throw a fit if I so much as touch a sword."

"He's just overprotective. You don't need to listen to the guy with a sister complex."

"I like him, so it doesn't matter."

A thought occurred to Edward as he watched the girl's pretty smile. *Maybe you would've liked to see this, but it's probably better that you can't. It'd only make you realize what you lost.*

"Oh, there he is. I'll get going now!"

"Slow down."

"I'm not a chi—"

"Oh, yes. You most definitely are a child."

Shea furrowed her eyebrows as soon as Sistina was out of sight. "Damn it."

Edward was so surprised when she clutched her head in pain and sank to the ground that he nearly approached her, even though he wouldn't have been able to catch her.

Shea muttered darkly through gritted teeth, "Damn you, I told you I didn't want to be your daughter. What's so wrong with that? If you force me to make this choice, it's not really a choice. Stop spewing nonsense."

Edward was at a loss for words, struck by the pure hatred in her voice. As Hayeon, she had often cursed, but never so viciously. Typically, she would give up on people rather than get angry with them. She despised wasting her energy.

"It's not like I get anything out of—yeah, right. I refuse. Stop being so clingy." She spat out the words and stomped off. Whatever was affecting her had stopped.

Even though this was a memory, Edward couldn't hear the other half of the conversation. Perhaps it was because there was no voice to be heard. Perhaps it was the voice of a god. Or perhaps she simply felt pain and heard no voice.

Other than moments like this, Shea's memories of her childhood were full of light.

"What do you think? It's good, isn't it?"

"Yup. My daughter is the best!"

"So, give up on the kitchen, mom."

"I can't do that."

"Oh, come on!" Even as she complained, her lips were always curled in a smile. She didn't want anything. In fact, she had so much that it was a problem.

The attention of Roux, for example. It was such a huge burden that it could've overshadowed everything else.

"Ugh. How did I end up like this?"

But Shea didn't seem to pay much attention to it. Maybe it was because Roux had offered her a choice, but he didn't seem to be able to force her to awaken to her special powers as much as he could pressure her. Most humans would have given in to that pressure.

Edward wondered why Roux had chosen her. She was charming, of course. But Edward was confident in saying that she wasn't someone who would bend to anyone's will, even if that person was a god. Shea never changed her mind once she had a firm opinion. It had been like that when she was Hayeon, too. That wouldn't have changed simply because she was now Shea.

So why had Shea given in?

CHAPTER SEVENTY-EIGHT

The reason Shea had given in was soon revealed.

"Who are you?" he asked.

"You're the one who came to see me. Shouldn't I be the one to ask you?"

"Oh, right. I'm Edward van Griffith."

"All right."

It was his younger self, holding her back as she tried to turn away. "What about you?"

She answered with a sigh, as if she'd rather not. "I'm Shea Grande."

She realized the truth as soon as she saw him. *Oh. Once again, I became a burden to you.*

She ran into her house and locked herself in her room.

Slam!

It was a while later that she finally let out her true feelings. "*Haha*, Gwonhyeok, you bastard." She kept laughing, weakly and sardonically.

Edward watched in silence, ignoring the fact that she'd insulted him and was now laughing at him. He knew this was her way of grieving.

"I don't deserve your love." She tried so hard to hold them back, but in the end, she couldn't stop the tears. "Why did you do it?"

Shea—no, Hayeon—was someone who could stand strong and keep on living, even if someone she loved died. But Gwonhyeok wasn't. It wasn't a difference in their love for each other, but a difference in their characters. She couldn't understand the boy who'd ended his own life to try and meet her again. And she couldn't accept it, either. The fact that he'd thrown everything away for her was overwhelming. And yet...

"And yet, you found me." Shea had to laugh at herself for being such a hypocrite for being happy that the boy she loved had done the unthinkable to see her again. She laughed and laughed, forgetting the tears that still flowed down her cheeks.

It was then that Edward realized she couldn't welcome his presence, as much as she'd missed him.

I must be tired... Am I seeing things?

Just as she hadn't looked entirely happy in his memory of their first meeting at Sangria. He hung his head at this harsh reality.

The memories that followed were of the Young Edward acting exactly as Edward expected himself to act.

"Shea."

"You're here again."

"Aren't you tired?"

"Here."

Edward squeezed his eyes shut at the antics of his younger self, which he didn't remember.

"Stop showing up."

But that wasn't the issue. He couldn't bear to watch himself bother her when he now knew that his presence wasn't entirely welcome. He was a burden. But even so, he felt strangely, selfishly satisfied with himself. "Do I make you uncomfortable?" *Even if I am a burden...*

"Will you stop coming if I say yes?"

...even if you don't welcome me...

"Of course not."

...letting you go was never an option for me.

Even if he'd somehow retained his memories and known the whole truth, he probably would've done the same thing. Because he'd found her, and he simply didn't know how to give up on her. Faced with his own selfishness, Edward smirked.

Shea, who'd been staring at Young Edward after his reply, burst out laughing. "*Ha! Haha. Ahahaha!*"

Edward sensed what this was about. He'd experienced this kind of outburst from her once before.

Shea continued to laugh out loud, even as Young Edward stared at her in confusion, until she finally smiled brightly and held up her hands in a gesture of surrender, just as Edward had expected. "All right, fine. I give up."

"...!"

He didn't know whether to laugh or cry as his younger self's eyes grew wide. He knew how precious that bliss was.

Shea gave him a lovely smile as she watched his face brighten, as if he'd gained the whole world. "How am I supposed to resist you?"

Edward could no longer hold back his tears as he heard her mumble this with a lovely smile. She was so wonderful for bearing with him, even though he was such a burden.

All right, I'll get lost in you one more time. Just like you did, long ago.

The days that followed were like a dream.

"Shea!"

"What took you so long?" She waited as he slowed to a stop before her. "Hey, did you run?"

"I wanted to see you sooner."

"You don't need to run."

"But I can't help it, Shea."

"Yeah, yeah. Let's go."

He ran as fast as he could to see her every time.

"How pretty!"

"Right? Here." He bought her whatever she looked at.

"...?!"

"You said you wanted it."

"I wasn't asking you to buy it for me," she scolded. "I have money too, you know."

"I know. But I wanted to get it for you anyway."

"Just this once, then."

The sight of them smiling at each other was the simple joy he had longed for. It was a perfect picture of a couple who loved each other above all else and were perfectly content with what they had.

Just like Gwonhyeok and Hayeon once were.

"Will you grant me the honor of being by your side for all eternity?"

"Whoa, how cheesy."

"..."

"Still, I love you."

The young man didn't regret even a second of the time it had taken to get his hands on this single pink rose when she responded with the loveliest smile. He gave her a kiss to convey his joy, and the young woman kissed him back, the most beautiful person in the world. It was perfect bliss that no one could ruin.

Only then did Edward realize the meaning behind what Shea had told him during the Glorious season.

"If you say those words, if you keep showing up, if you keep acting like this..."

"..."

"...The resolve I made..."

"..."

"...becomes useless."

Ah, I see. It's just as you said.

He hadn't changed. He'd even said the exact same words years later, as he professed his feelings to her during the Glorious season. Even if he'd retained his memory of the past, it would've been hard to repeat himself word for word. But because he knew what was about to happen, it was even more heartbreaking. And yet, he wished that their happiness would last a bit longer.

But it came to an end far too quickly.

The end snuck up on them without warning. Just as they were enjoying each other's presence without a care in the world, the young man suddenly coughed up blood.

Cough.

"Ed!" Shea's eyes widened at the sudden sight of the red liquid.

Edward had never seen her look so shocked, not ever. She hurried to his side, panicked.

Young Edward had eyes only for her and how worried she looked, even though he'd coughed up blood. But then he began to throw up blood clots without pausing.

"Blaaargh."

Edward watched in awe, having never seen a single human expel so much blood. As he observed Shea seemingly trying to catch the blood Young Edward was throwing up, perhaps to put it back, he realized that he was currently completely fine. He felt stupid for not realizing it sooner because he'd been watching Shea the entire time. The Shea Grande he knew was exactly that kind of person.

"Ed! Ed! Stay with me!" She cupped the blood he was throwing up in her hands and used her divine powers to check his vitals.

Even as she saw the truth, she couldn't believe it. She denied reality. His fate, which had been fine a moment ago, was suddenly running out. As much as fate had no master, this was completely unnatural. No god could manage something like this.

Shea concluded that her imperfect powers had misinterpreted things. She caught him as he lost consciousness and continued to use her powers to read his fate, never giving up. And in the end, she gave in and activated her true powers, going against her own convictions.

Whoosh.

A divine breeze enveloped her, and golden light radiated from her hand. It was a level of divine power beyond what even blessed priests could achieve. It was astounding that she possessed such immense power, even though her God-given abilities had yet to fully awaken. This was proof of her uniqueness and how dearly she was cherished by Roux.

As she waited for a miracle to happen, her eyes shot open as if something unbelievable had happened. Young Edward wasn't getting any better. Although she remembered her past life, she was still very young, and so instead of trying to figure out what was wrong, she panicked and continued to try her powers. But the result she was hoping for refused to happen.

It was then that she realized why.

She sounded certain as she looked up at the sky. "It's *you*."

Though anyone would say it was insane, twisted affection was still affection.

He answered her, though she didn't welcome it one bit. *"This time, it wasn't me."*

The Children of God were unfortunate because they were loved by Roux. It was a reality Shea was learning to accept, and she refused to believe the voice. "Yeah, right. Who else would—"

Roux answered her in all sincerity. *"This is the price that this boy decided to pay in exchange for meeting you again. It wouldn't usually be this harsh, but this boy's father sold his own son to bring his beloved back to life. This boy is simply paying the price. It has nothing to do with me."*

CHAPTER
SEVENTY-NINE

It was a perfectly logical explanation that was hard to refute, but Shea wasn't fooled. *I'm not that naive.* "Even that must have been your doing. You're the only god in this world who can make someone pay such a price."

It wasn't as if there were any gods in this world who could offer to bring someone back to life for a price. Those who didn't know any of this might've been fooled, but not Shea. She'd gone around to find the other Children of God in order to try and get rid of her own powers. This was why she knew the others, even though her powers hadn't awakened properly yet.

The Great God Roux looked at Shea with a blank face at her interrogating question. *"It was his choice."*

"Sure, of course it was," Shea shot back, enunciating every word clearly. "But that doesn't exonerate you for what you did."

Roux waited in silence, knowing that he would soon hear from her mouth the words he wanted to hear.

In the end, she gave in and spoke them. "What do I have to do?"

"If you give up on him, you may live the life you always dreamed of."

"Stop giving me options I can't choose." She chuckled darkly, muttering about why her god was so cruel as to always offer options she couldn't choose. "You win, father. I'll do as you wish."

Shea looked bitter and lonely as she admitted her defeat, but she had a satisfied look in her eyes as if she were glad to have something worth sacrificing for.

Don't do it... Edward begged her soundlessly. He wished he could run to her to tell her not to do it, that she didn't need to. That he wasn't worth it. He wanted to argue with her, to demand why she was sacrificing herself to save him when he was nothing but a burden. He'd realized so many times now how little he deserved her, how unworthy he was of her, and he couldn't keep being so shameless. But he had never imagined, not once in his whole life, that he had been this heavy a burden to her.

For the first time, Roux' voice rang out in a divine word passed down to Shea.

"It is not enough. Even if you awaken to your powers and officially become my child, it is not enough to pay the full price."

Shea let out a loud, cynical laugh at his cold, arrogant words. "Wow, how greedy of you."

His greed was so vast that it could cover the whole world. She couldn't understand how anyone could consider this god to be merciful.

She cursed him inwardly, but she'd already made her decision. It hadn't been much of a decision to make. The answer had been set from the start.

"I'll give you my love," she said calmly. "I'll give it all to you. I've already given it all to this man, so I don't have anyone else to give it to. I'll give it all to you."

Then she smiled. It was a lovely, heartbreaking smile.

And with that smile, her god gave her an answer. *"The deal has been made. You will have to honor this covenant."*

"It's not like you'll give me a choice."

That threat meant nothing. She was sure that she wouldn't meet him ever again. Her father and her fate would see to it.

A light began to emanate from her. As it transferred to Young Edward, her true divine power began to activate.

As she watched his life return to him, Shea said the words she'd somehow never been able to say to his face. "I love you."

"..."

"I think I loved you from the moment I saw you. And..."

"..."

"...I was so happy that you came all the way here to see me again."

A single tear rolled down the bridge of her nose and dropped onto Edward's cheek.

And at that moment, his body began to fade along with the light. His fate was being reversed. Her covenant would be fulfilled. Knowing that she would never see him again and that even if she did, he wouldn't be the man who loved her, Shea tried to let go of everything.

Rustle.

"..."

And with that, Edward disappeared, along with the light.

Only Shea was left.

She sat in that empty field a long time, not sure what she was looking at. And after some time had passed, Edward, who'd been watching in silence, slowly stepped closer.

There had been countless times when he wanted to step in and interfere, but believing they were the Shea of the past, he had held back. This was the first time he had stepped forward.

He sensed that now was the time to move. It was almost instinctive. The Shea in front of him now was the woman he loved—the woman he'd been searching for.

Tap.

Rustle.

Just as he reached her, the young Shea turned into the older Shea he knew.

And he realized he'd been a fool. The Shea he'd watched this whole time was the Shea he'd been looking for all along. The real Shea, the Shea he was supposed to find, had taken the opportunity her meddling siblings had given him to show him her past and answer the question he'd always had.

There had been all kinds of illogical holes in the explanation he'd accepted without suspicion. Even if the two other Children of God had used their own powers, it made no sense that he would see Shea's memories without her permission.

"You could have run away halfway through, but you stayed until the end."

Edward felt he would burst into tears again at the sound of her voice. "You know I would never run away."

How could I? He'd known from the start that she would let him out of her mind if he refused to watch more of her memories at any point. But the thought of leaving hadn't even occurred. All this was about her, so how could he have run away? He felt the same, even now that he'd seen everything.

He didn't regret it one bit.

He didn't regret falling in love with her again, either.

Shea smiled in a self-deprecating way, as if she knew what he was thinking even though she wasn't looking at him. "I saved your life in exchange for my love."

"You did."

"You might resent me for it, but I will never regret it."

She knew. She knew that he would rather die than give up on her. But Shea wasn't like that. She would rather give up her love than let him die.

Edward sank to his knees in front of her, after she professed her love to him in this way. He took her hands and raised them to his face. "I know. You're Shea Grande. It's all right. You can do whatever you want. Even if you leave me behind, I'll come find you time and time again. I've done it before."

"Idiot."

"You say that like you only just realized it. I've always been like this, Hayeon."

"*Hahaha!*" She burst out laughing brightly at his teary words and his sad smile. She laughed as if she was the happiest person in the world.

"This is why I can't stop myself from falling in love with you." She spoke the sweetest words in the world with the most delightful smile, as she gave him a lovely kiss.

This woman was pure perfection. Edward kissed her back with reverence, as if he were worshipping her.

He didn't care about the crazy things he'd done. He was capable of doing whatever crazy things were necessary, from here on out. He was certain of it.

Because he'd been saved by this one kiss.

"Let's go back, Ed."

"All right. Let's go back, Shea."

With those last words, the past and her memories faded. And when he slowly opened his eyes...

"Welcome back, Shea."

...his whole world also opened her eyes.

"Shea!"

"Ow, my ears. I don't have hearing problems yet, you know."

"Look at that attitude. She just woke up, too."

"What in the world does her boyfriend see in her?"

"No idea. He must be as crazy as her."

"You're right, he didn't seem normal."

She covered her ears at the chatter greeting her return.

Noise stuttered, with clear hurt in his eyes at her cold response. "You... You're such... You're such a bitch."

"So?" *Did you find that out just now?* She couldn't see why he seemed so surprised.

She shook her head, mumbling how she couldn't understand them even after all these years, and then began to pretend to miss her lover, who'd left the room to bring her food.

Noise tutted at her, immediately realizing what she was looking forward to. "Just look at that. She's looking forward to food more than her boyfriend, who risked his life to bring her back."

"All right, you can starve."

"It would be very un-Korean of me to skip a meal."

He immediately stopped complaining, apparently unwilling to forgo a meal.

Tap, tap, tap.

"Hmm?"

"He's here."

"My food is here?"

"No, not food. It's your boyfriend."

Everyone rushed down the stairs at the sound of footsteps outside, pretending to look forward to seeing Edward, when they were looking forward to food, but...

Cough.

"..."

They were met with a sight they hadn't even imagined was possible.

"Ed."

Cough.

Shea caught Edward as he began to collapse. "Noise!"

"I'm calling them."

"Use your powers," she cried desperately, scooping up the blood that was pooling on the ground and pouring it back into Edward, as if this would fix him.

Noise, also panicking, said words he immediately regretted saying. "You should use yours. What am I supposed to do? You're the one with the life-saving power."

She was the only one with the power to save him.

Shea froze, looking devastated, silently crying. No tears were flowing—she had no tears left to cry—yet she wailed in utter despair through her smile. "It's not working."

"..."

"I've been trying to use my power this whole time, but it won't work."

"Lariana."

"Why? Why does it never work on the people I want to save?"

Her whole body was breaking down. She was completely shutting down. Though she was covered in blood, Noise wrapped her in a tight embrace. It was the only comfort he could offer her, despite his many years of experience.

"There were so few of them. I could count them on one hand. They were mine. Why won't it work?"

"Don't cry, Shea." *You're going to make me cry, so please don't.*

Eid came running toward them, his face contorted in a grimace. "Maxwell!"

"..."

Only then did Shea look up at the cause of all this: Duke Maxwell. The hypocrite, Maxwell.

She couldn't say anything. She couldn't even ask him how he had dared to stab this precious man. She couldn't even feel the anger. Perhaps it was because her fury was so great that she was incapable of feeling anything.

"Ha!" Duke Maxwell let out a laugh as he watched the man who was no doubt here to kill him. He looked like he couldn't be happier about it. As Eid's sword reached his neck, he spoke his last words. "I kept my promise, my—"

"..."

Shing.

Splatter.

Blood exploded like a fountain.

Shea seemed entirely uninterested in the fact that she had nearly been doused in blood. She stared down at the head rolling on the ground as if she were in a daze.

Though the others seemed not to have heard, Shea had heard every word.

He said, "My God."

And the voice she despised and yet loved so much rang out inside her head. *"My foolish daughter. Your mistake has forced me to dirty my own hands."*

"..."

She drew Edward's sword, lightning quick.

"Wait—"

"She's insane!"

"Shea!"

But the blade was faster than those trying to stand in its way. The sword rapidly approached Shea's neck.

"Lariana!" With one last cry, they anticipated the awful tragedy that was about to happen.

But it didn't.

A blindingly bright golden light appeared and formed into a hand that stopped her sword.

As soon as they saw it, all his children there recognized it. Though they'd never seen him, though they resented and loved him, they knew this was their "father."

The daughter their father loved most faced him for the second time. She let out an empty laugh. "I knew you'd come. You won't even let me die."

"Foolish child. He isn't worth anything."

"He is my everything. You know this." She dropped to her knees and clung to her father's leg.

"..."

Those gathered were struck silent with awe when they saw her act in a way they never would've expected this prideful woman to act. It was as if she had no pride anymore.

"Father, this is my life's wish. Your daughter is begging you. I'll do anything you want, give you anything you ask me to give."

"..."

"So please, please give me one more chance."

"..."

"Save him, father. I'm begging you."

Shea cried as she pleaded with him, putting down every last shred of her dignity.

Even the most heartless person would have been moved by her desperation, but this only angered their father.

He looked down at her with disgust and raised his voice. "I have already given you every chance. I have brought him back to life once already—because you begged me to. And you still won't give up on him? How dare you!"

As his wrath fell on her like a lightning bolt, Shea convulsed in agony. "How am I supposed to give up on him?"

"..."

His eyes widened, as if he'd never expected Shea to talk back to him.

But Shea had a lot to say. Too much.

CHAPTER
EIGHTY

The words she'd wanted to give voice to so often but held back countless times burst forth like water through a broken dam. "You know... You know I tried. I tried so hard, but..."

"..."

"What am I supposed to do when he keeps coming back?"

"..."

"Even when he loses his memory, even when he's reborn, he keeps coming back to me. What am I supposed to do with him?"

"Lariana."

"Father, why didn't you erase my memory instead of his? Why did you leave my memory intact? You could've kept me from falling in love with him again, if you hated him that much."

Then this never would have happened, and it would've been so much easier. Everyone knew this. Even he probably knew this. And yet, that wasn't what he'd done, because if he had, she would no longer have been the daughter he loved.

"Never once have I wanted your love or your powers," she cried. "You know this damn well. The only thing I ever wanted was this man!"

He'd given it all to her without her consent, then made her responsible for it. He made her pay the price. *How terribly ironic.* She'd endured because she had someone she loved and wanted to protect. But without him in this world, she had no reason to endure any of it.

"Give him back. Give him back to me. The man I love... please give him back."

"..."

"I don't need to be your daughter. I don't need your love... You can take it all away..."

"..."

"So please give him back to me."

She had been in such denial, so selfish, that while she'd begged her god to save this man before, she'd never declared that she didn't need anything else.

Her father looked down at her and mumbled to himself. "Foolish girl..."

"..."

"As if love is worth all this."

She nearly burst out laughing. It was funny coming from him—when he'd ruined her life in the name of love. As laughable and pathetic as it was, she couldn't say that he was entirely wrong. She, too, had ruined someone's life in the name of love—only now was she able to face the truth. And along with it, she was able to make a resolution: to ruin her own life as well, since she'd ruined his.

"Your daughter begs you one last time." She would probably never be able to ask him for anything again.

"…"

 "Please. Disown me."

Relief flooded over her. She should've done this from the start. She'd taken the long way around—when she could've done this.

He sounded defeated. "They say no parent can persuade their child to change their mind."

He disappeared, leaving behind residual spots of light.

"…"

And as the last of that light disappeared, her wish was fulfilled, the wish she'd had all her life.

Tears traveled down her cheeks. She could finally cry to her heart's content.

Her hair and eyes turned black. It was Shea Grande as she was supposed to be, without the colors given to her by divine powers but the colors she inherited from her parents.

"Your hair. Your eyes!"

"It's fine." They didn't seem to believe her, but Shea basked in the miracle, smiling the happiest smile they'd ever seen as she pressed her lips against Edward's hand. "Father..."

"..."

"He finally gave up on me."

And only then, after she had let go of everything and returned to the person she was meant to be, could she finally reach for the future she had hoped for.

"I love you."

"Shea."

"Welcome back, Ed."

Welcome to the rest of our lives together.

"Lariana!"

"That's not my name anymore."

As soon as they sensed the change, the people who'd rarely visited even when she invited them crowded around to see her. The house bustled with activity as guest after guest arrived.

"Hey!"

"Did you finally do it?"

"You're insane!"

"Wow, family really is good."

They were all here to check on her.

As Shea gave them a carefree smile, her siblings tried to shake her, deadly serious, although they would've smiled back at any other time.

"You shouldn't be laughing right now! How is your body?"

"Is your divine power gone?"

"Part of the price you paid was the inability to change your hair and eye colors. They're back to black now, so it does seem like it's gone."

"No, you never know," said Petra, who may have believed Shea but didn't trust their father. "Our *dear* father would never give up on her so easily."

The rest of them agreed, and they continued to solemnly check Shea for signs of foul play. Shea, who would otherwise have struggled to get away, stayed still and let them get a good look at her.

The person who finally calmed them down was Solomon, whom they never imagined would come here of his own accord. "You really did it. Congratulations."

"Thanks. I feel a little bad for getting out of it alone, though."

"You haven't gotten out fully. In exchange for losing your divine powers, you..." He trailed off, finding it difficult to voice the hard truth.

But Shea finished the sentence for him. "I'll live a shorter life than most humans. And I'll probably get dragged off as soon as I die."

"And you don't mind?"

She'd only just found happiness, but it would be cut short sooner rather than later. Of course she wasn't completely fine with it. No human would be content with that. But for Shea, a short but free life was preferable to a long life in shackles.

"It's much better than living in debt for years on end, without ever knowing when you will die," she said. "A long life means nothing to most of us. Even if it's shorter than the average lifespan, I'll at least make it to fifty. That's enough."

It was more than enough. She had never been able to spend that many years with him before. The promise of spending those years together now was more than enough for her.

"All right. If you're happy, my dear."

"I'll keep running the café, so visit me any time."

"Of course. I can't live without having your food once in a while."

And she had people who cared for her. She was blessed without a doubt.

Once she'd sent them home and was left alone, the person Shea had been waiting for finally came to see her—the person who hadn't been able to move on because of her lover and because of her son, even though she'd made the decision herself. Shea had sensed her presence all this time, though she hadn't acknowledged it.

"Sistina."

"Shea! You realized right away that it's time for me to move on, didn't you?"

"I did. How else could I be brave enough to call you?" She'd known that the next time she called her would be the last time.

"Haha. You're known for your coolness, though."

"Not cool enough to treat you like that when you're dead." She hadn't been able to face Sistina when she'd failed to save her. She'd tried to bring her back to life using her powers, but it hadn't worked because of the strong chains of fate surrounding her.

"It wasn't your fault." Sistina smiled that lovely smile of hers, as if none of that bothered her.

Shea smiled back almost reflexively, as she'd always done. "Your son turned out like you, despite my best efforts."

"Nah. He's a lot like you."

"No, he's not. No matter how much I tried to brainwash him, his instincts are like yours. I tried so hard not to turn him into a pushover like you."

"Hahaha. Eid would be happy to hear that."

"He wouldn't care what Elias was like." *He's your son, after all.*

Eid Roux Vencroft was complete trash who didn't treat others like fellow human beings, although he'd been completely different with Sistina. Then again, perhaps Sistina had been the only person worth calling a human in his life. And then he'd lost everything.

"I'm not going to do anything for Eid Roux Vencroft," Shea declared. It wasn't like she could do anything for him anymore, anyway. She still had plenty of people she could ask for favors, but she didn't want to.

Sistina nodded, as if she hadn't doubted that Shea would feel this way. *"I know."*

"Aren't you disappointed?"

"What? Of course not." Sistina shook her head, asking when she'd ever been disappointed in Shea and giving Shea a kind smile. *"I've always been grateful to you."*

“…”

“You did more than enough for me.”

“What did I ever do for you?”

“A lot.” Sistina chuckled, pointing out that Shea never remembered what she did. *“I’m here to say goodbye one last time. It’s your turn to be happy now.”*

“Sistina.”

“Be happy, Shea. Be happy, for my sake.”

“…”

“Thank you for everything.” And with one last smile, she disappeared.

As always, Shea didn’t get the chance to stop her. Left alone once again, she smiled as she recalled her friend’s smile. “I was going to do that even without you telling me.”

Next time. I’m over it.

Inside Edward’s office, documents and reports had piled so high that they seemed in danger of collapsing.

“Do you have no shame, Ed?” Shea stared at the astounding amount of paper in the room.

“I think the emperor is the one without any shame,” Edward responded with a sob. She’d finally begun to find happiness, but his damn friend had buried him in work. This wasn't entirely Eid's fault, because the empire had fallen into an emergency state, but Edward still blamed Eid. "Shea, could you go and tell him off for me?" He never would've asked for such a favor normally, but this was bad.

But Shea, who had no pity for her boyfriend, shook her head. "Nope. I don't even want to see his face."

It's his fault that my friend is gone. It wasn't as though she despised the man, but Shea had no love to spare for him either. Her answer was final.

Edward hadn't expected her to agree, so he wasn't hurt. He sighed and went back to work.

Shea poked through the documents with vague interest. "There won't be any more natural disasters. It's just that the blessing is gone. Cedric said he'd stop, too."

He looked up. "You talked to him?"

"Yup. He came to see me yesterday."

After she'd seen Sistina off, she opened the door to find Cedric standing there. He'd heard everything. When he concluded that Sistina had finally left, he turned away from Shea without a word, very much relieved. Though she didn't know what he would do with his life from now on, she knew he wouldn't die. Sistina wouldn't have wanted that.

"That annoying Vencroft blessing is finally gone. Eid must be happy."

"I'm not sure about that. It's a result of his lover's sacrificing her life, so he can't be too happy about it."

Sistina had chosen this fate for Eid's sake. If she hadn't died, things wouldn't have gone this way. The child blessed by Roux with the ability to predict the future came to this conclusion. That was why she couldn't be saved. It was also the reason why Shea couldn't entirely hate Eid.

"Anyway," she added, "you should ask him if he wants to see his son."

Edward jumped to his feet, disregarding the piles of paper in danger of collapse. "Can he?" He seemed to be in disbelief.

Shea laughed out loud. "Whatever our happy ending may be, we should try to go toward it now." *If only for those who sacrificed themselves for us.*

"The same goes for us, right?"

Her smile was brighter than a spring morning. "I'm going to strive to be happy from now on. Always."

"..."

"We have to spend every precious moment doing our best. We've endured so much for so long."

"You're right." He looked at her as if her radiant smile was blinding him—before he smiled as well.

Shea took his hands in hers and squeezed them tightly. "Let's keep going together."

...Toward our happy ending.

The End.